EWAN

UNCHARTED WATERS

Published in the UK in 2022 by ScottBurn Press

Copyright © Murray Campbell 2022

Murray Campbell has asserted his right under the
Copyright, Designs and Patents Act, 1988, to be identified
as the author of this work.

Paperback ISBN 978-1-8383840-3-6
eBook ISBN 978-1-8383840-4-3

Cover design and typeset by SpiffingCovers

EWAN
UNCHARTED WATERS

MURRAY CAMPBELL

To SDS
"Where are you going?"

CHAPTER 1

Saturday morning, the first of January, started normally for the day after typical Scottish New Year celebrations. Ewan's mum and dad leave to drive over to see a bed-bound cousin that lived on the other side of the bay, so Ewan pops next door to see his mate, Fred. They settle in the kitchen, which is littered with plates of half-eaten sandwiches and dubious dollops of haggis.

"Right, you two, I need to get cracking. Go and play in the front room and take Daniel Dog with you. I don't want him tempted by all this food. And leave the piano alone; I can't stand the awful noise you make trying to play 'Chopsticks'." Ewan knew that Fred's mother had been a renowned concert pianist at the Inverness Philharmonic; she often said so. The front room boasted a grand piano that jostled with a three-piece suite for room. The highlight of the year for both families was yesterday, Hogmanay, when the sitting room had echoed to the strains of Scottish melodies and the raised voices of distant cousins who probably only came for the free food and booze. Ewan spent the evening rescuing Fred from unthoughtful relatives who tried to talk down to him when Ewan knew he was a damn sight more intelligent than any of them; hiding in Fred's bedroom, they played video games, at which Fred always excelled. Ewan was a bad loser; he didn't appreciate Fred's mathematical brain; well not until many years later when Fred's autism was fully explained to him, a word never mentioned in conversation. Ewan had often overheard the parents murmur to outsiders that their relationship didn't need any labels, and neither Ewan nor Fred recognised their difference; they just grew up together, Ewan as a friend, and Fred as an extraordinary friend, who was always the brightest brain in the school.

It was one day short of Ewan's tenth birthday. Having been banished from the kitchen, they were in Fred's front room with their homework lying on the floor. It was a routine they followed to anchor Fred's autism. They had been chums for as long as Ewan could remember. There was a difference between them. Fred was always neat and tidy; Ewan was scruffy at the edges. Both had doting parents; both were "only-childs". They lived next door to one another on the same street, and the families enjoyed an open-door existence. Their adjacent bungalows on Nigg View were built of pink granite and had panoramic bay windows with a magnificent and magnetic view from their cliff-top setting of Nigg Bay on the Cromarty Firth in Scotland.

Fred had a Labrador puppy called Daniel, and it always produced a calming effect on him when the dog's cold wet nose found its target. The three of them went for long walks or bike rides, and the dog instinctively knew Fred's moods. Ewan probably talked to Daniel more than he did Fred, but Fred would benefit from the conversation and occasionally butt in. Nothing moved on Nigg Bay that could escape their notice, and Fred was addicted to his telescope. Sometimes his running commentary was like a chant, but Ewan had become used to it, as he had to many of Fred's habits. His mother, Mrs Oliphant, knew the burden of keeping Fred safe and was forever saying how grateful she was to Ewan.

Both of them were lying on the floor in the front room with Ewan trying to finish his homework. "Fred, I'm stuck on the equation. I get X to be two different numbers."

"Well, they can be if you've used different values, but the relationship stays the same."

"So, what is the point of working it out? Why do we bother?"

"Because that's how we do algebra. Here, look at mine." As Fred passed the jotter over, Ewan heard the noise of a car on the gravel drive, and, in a flash, Daniel was up at the bay window wagging his tail. They both jostled with one another to be second to see what had made the noise. A police car was drawing up to the house, and they exchanged glances.

"Fred, have you been up to no good? There are two of them, and one is a woman."

"Not me. I'm always on time with my homework." Ewan smiled. There was a pure innocence about Fred that touched Ewan deeply.

"Let's see what's up." As they reached the corridor, they heard whispering, with Fred's mum repeating, "No, no, no," in a scared voice. Ewan walked towards her. She looked white as a sheet.

"What's the matter? Fred's a little anxious. He says he's done nothing wrong."

"Ewan, these officers have something to tell you. Please

go into the kitchen with them; I'll keep Fred in the front room."

As the officers in their black uniforms led Ewan into the kitchen, he was trying desperately to think what he had done wrong, so he could get his excuses in order. The woman police officer spoke first.

"Ewan, we have some sad news for you. There's been an accident. Your mum and dad were in their car when a lorry hit them. We don't know any more than that, but they didn't survive the accident. Now, we know this will be difficult for you to take in or understand. Your Aunt Bessie is on her way to take you home, and she will explain what happened in more detail. We're very, very sorry to bring you this news. If you feel like crying, go ahead. Mrs Oliphant will look after you for now. Fred will be told, so you don't have to tell him."

The male officer put his hand on Ewan's shoulder. "My heart goes out to you. I have a son your age, and I can't think how he would react. The pain of your loss will ease over time, I promise. Just keep your happy memories at the front of your thoughts. Be brave."

As the police left, Mrs Oliphant entered the kitchen with Fred, who gave Ewan a hug, something he never did. Ewan was thinking how much he needed Fred to be with him now when Mrs Oliphant interrupted his thoughts. "Ewan, would you like your usual cup of tea and scone?"

"I think so. What about my birthday party tomorrow? Dad said it took him ages to find ten candles. What happens now?"

"Well, we'll talk that through with your Aunt Bessie. She is on her way and can tell you more when she gets here.

Go and play your video game with Fred in the front room. I'll get the tea."

As Ewan entered the front room, Fred rushed over and hugged him again, leaving Ewan perplexed. Fred and Ewan were always physically close, but on a different level. Fred was a stumbler in many things. Ewan had to catch him or let him fall if he wasn't in danger. It was as if Fred felt he was always invincible, and Ewan knew he wasn't. The scraped knees, bloody shirts, and torn trainers always attested to some wayward moment that Ewan couldn't predict. It was a strange relationship, but it worked, and seemed to give Ewan responsibility that he liked.

"Let's play that car-racing game. I need something to occupy my mind."

They took up their play consoles. Fred stopped and turned to face Ewan. "Look, you've always got me to play with."

"I know I have, Fred, but I'm a bit numb at the moment, and I have butterflies in my tummy. Let's just play the game. I don't want to talk."

Aunt Bessie popped her head round the sitting-room door and said a quiet "hello". Ewan dropped his play-station and walked slowly over. They hugged. "Ewan, how are you?"

"I don't know. Is it true? Were Mum and Dad in an accident?"

"Sadly, yes, and it wasn't their fault. I've come to look after you. We will both have to be brave. I've spoken to Uncle Frank who's in Inverness, so he'll be here in a couple of hours. I'm going to sleep in your house for the next few days, so nothing much will change. You'll sleep in your normal bed, and I'll make sure you have plenty to eat. You've always said you like my 'tattie scones' so I'll make plenty. We'll try and keep to your normal routine, and you will be with Fred as usual. I know this is going to be an abrupt change for you, and I know you will be ten tomorrow. I'll bake a special cake for you, if you help me."

"I always help you with the icing. Dad has some candles for the cake. They're in the kitchen drawer next to the knives."

"Okay. Remember, your uncle and I don't have any children of our own, so you'll make a perfect substitute," she said blinking back tears. "We'll be surrogate parents. It will be a challenge for us oldies, so we'll need your help. Mrs Oliphant won't change anything. Just tell us if you get upset. What do you say?"

"Sounds okay to me, but what's a 'surrogate'?"

"It means we'll be stand-ins. Is that okay?"

"Yup. Shall we go next door and start the cake?"

"Yes, and you can bring Fred and Daniel with you." She was Ewan's favourite aunt. It would be a start, at least.

"And make sure that dog doesn't lick the spoon."

CHAPTER 2

"All rise," boomed the voice of the court usher. The jury filed into their seats self-consciously, staring at the floor. The room was all glass and light oak, with no dark shadows, no hiding places. A huge crest clung to the wall above the judge's seat. This was Aberdeen's High Criminal Court at Mercatgate. To Ewan, everything looked so clinical. Everyone's face was glum, and black cloaks, topped by white wigs, appeared like menacing birds. The spectacle was new and a little scary to him, but they had said attendance at the proceedings would give him closure, whatever that meant. He thought all the doors seemed to manage to close on their own.

He was dressed in his Sunday best with his dark grey suit, brilliant white shirt, and burgundy school tie, which Aunt Bessie had to knot after many tries by Ewan. His seat had a plastic covering that made his backside stick to it, and if he moved, it made an embarrassing squeaky sound. He coughed each time he moved to disguise any possible farting noises. He wanted to be anonymous and any staring in his direction would turn him bright red. He was sitting alongside a lady lawyer whom he liked; her name was Mary. The table was huge and littered with stacks of books.

"I'll try and explain what's going on. We are here in what is called the well of the court. Those people that shuffled in are the jury. The man in the big chair under the crest is the judge, and he wears that bright red coat to signify his authority," Mary whispered behind her cupped hand.

"But why does he wear such a long wig? Won't it stop him hearing what's being said?"

"Don't worry; he is a wily old codger, who doesn't miss a trick, and he has eyes in the back of his head. Nothing gets past him. We have to sit here while he goes through the procedure we talked about. Remember, you have nothing to worry about, and you're fairly well hidden behind our stack of folders and evidence boxes. If you want, I can get you a cushion so you can see better."

"No, it's okay. I can see enough." Ewan regretted turning down the offer after another fart-like sound escaped from his chair.

Ewan tried to keep up with the continuous ebb and flow of conversation but couldn't help his mind wandering. Occasionally, the judge looked in his direction, as if knowing that Ewan wasn't paying too much attention. Sometimes the look seemed to be asking him for a reply, and he was tempted to give his two-penny worth, but he had been told to only speak if he was ever asked a direct question. They briefed him that the judge would ask him to give his thoughts, but they never said when that would happen. He had a speech made up and hoped his mind wouldn't go blank on him at the critical moment.

The proceedings for the first two days were very much stop-start. Quite a few times the jury trooped out, which

Mary said was to allow the lawyers to discuss a point of law. Ewan counted fifteen people in what Mary described as the juror's box. They mainly looked at whoever was talking, but every now and then, when his parents were mentioned, he was the target of their gaze, and he attempted to shrink into his seat. When there were descriptions of the accident, Ewan didn't look at the diagrams that popped up on a giant screen. At times, the voices were just a babble of noise. He found himself trying to remember what his mum and dad looked like; it was a strange feeling as the images formed and disappeared. He thought of Fred, whose daily timetable would have been interrupted, leaving him lost, and Ewan felt a pang of guilt that he wasn't there for him. Fred relished habit and the security it gave him. They, unknowingly, provided a crutch for each other, with Fred's mother sewing their routines together, and a helping hand from Daniel's big tongue.

On the third day, Mary stopped Ewan before entering the courtroom.

"Ewan, today is very important. What will happen is that the judge will sum up everything relevant that has been said. You know you've already prepared your statement and that you want to read it out. I think that's a good idea as long as you still feel comfortable. You address yourself to the judge. He'll ask you for it directly."

"I'm fine. Just tell me when to expect it."

The hubbub was just dying down as the court usher rose up once again, like a perennial jack-in-the-box. "All rise." The judge took his seat, and there was some bowing to one another at the front. Ewan didn't join in, but Mary did. The court usher, a very tall man who Ewan thought looked like the undertaker from the funeral proceedings, turned and faced the jury box. "Foreman of the jury, have you reached a verdict and is it the verdict of you all?" A portly gentleman stood up. "Yes, we have," he tried to intone, but his voice was squeaky and lost some authority. Ewan imagined it was Minnie Mouse replying to Mickey. If both the foreman and judge possessed big black ears, Ewan thought it would have played better. Fred and he were avid fans of the cartoons.

"Do you find the defendant guilty or not guilty?"

"Guilty, and that is the verdict of us all."

There was complete silence in the room. The prisoner in the dock put his head in his hands and his shoulders were heaving. The judge turned to look directly at Ewan. "I believe we have a witness impact statement." Mary stood up, and the plastic squeaking sound caught Ewan by surprise. He struggled to suppress a giggle, thinking maybe she should have had a cushion.

"M'lord, the sole family survivor, the son, has a prepared statement, a copy of which we have lodged."

"Please tell him to go ahead and speak in his own time at his own pace."

Mary prompted Ewan to stand up and gave him the white card on which he had written his thoughts.

"Young man, just take your time. I am here to listen to you."

Ewan began. "I have been angry since the accident. I had a lot of dreams, but they have gone. I try not to dream any more. Dad was going to take me to the Bay to see the new rigs. It was going to be my birthday present. That will never happen. That makes me angry. My mum made the best scones ever, and I helped her. That will never happen again. When I've nothing else to do, I try and blot out all my memories 'cos they make me cry, but it's bloody difficult. I now swear a lot, and I know it's bad, but I'm still angry. All my dreams have been killed. That's it."

"Thank you for that, young man. It was a very brave thing to do. Eventually, you will learn better words to express yourself, but swear-words will do for now. You can sit down again."

Ewan took his seat with angry tears in his eyes and a very red face. Cathartic it might have been, but he felt untold pain inside. The judge called the court to order. Some of the jurors were crying.

"Prisoner in the dock, you have been found guilty of the offence of death by dangerous driving in that you crashed into a vehicle that was lawfully on the highway, whilst you were texting on your phone, and records show that you had been doing so for over an hour. By this act, you killed a mother and father, destroyed a family unit, and left a ten-year-old boy an orphan. You have previous convictions for illegal use of your phone when driving. You failed to learn your lesson. As a warning to others and specifically to you, you will go to prison for ten years, with your licence suspended for a similar period. Remember, you have given a boy a life sentence without his parents. Take him down."

Ewan was ushered out, guarded by Mary and his uncle and aunt, to begin his own sentence.

CHAPTER 3

He sat at a familiar kitchen table while a couple of his aunts and uncles discussed his future, as if he wasn't there. He drummed on the table with his knuckles in time to the incessant ticking of the pendulum clock.

"Ewan, must you?" It was the ever-proper Aunt Tilda.

"Well, I'm sitting here while you argue about where I shall go and what I should do. How about asking me? I've overheard you say that you can't work out why I'm so angry and withdrawn. It's 'cos I'm being ignored. Mum used to say that the road to heaven is paved with good intentions, and most of them get lost to memory before the first step is taken. You mention time and again that it will be for my own good, but I have decided that I want to have a say."

"Now, now, Ewan. Uncle Frank and Aunt Bessie want you to have a home where you can mend. We have all lost something precious, and although we don't show it, we hurt as well. Yes, you're right. We need to ask what you want to do."

"Well, I've studied hard and been reading books by the barrowload. It's kept my mind off other things. And escaping with Fred to his dad's boatyard has kept us both out of trouble. With the boats up on stilts for cleaning,

Fred and I have been studying the barnacles that have to be cleaned off; we're now barnacle experts."

"We're glad you enjoy going to the boatyard. Fred's dad is proud of how you help out."

"We help where we can with the cleaning. Fred said we should go in for boat-spotting just as people go in for trainspotting, and he's become clued up on the different shapes of the hulls. Now he's become an expert, or so he says, on their different strakes, flukes, and designs, and because I have to listen to him, I can become an expert too, though I think I'm spouting gibberish when I repeat what he says. You should see the amount of books he takes from the library. He's a fast reader, and it's rubbing off on me. A lot of it is over my head when he talks about things like fluid dynamics, thermodynamics, electronics, and computers; Fred has told me to memorise these names, but I can only just remember them and don't really know what they mean, but, if anyone knows, it's Fred. He's said he'll help me and has drawn up what he calls a simple computer programme that he has on his laptop and quizzes me on our bike rides, so I am learning, slowly. I like playing with the computer."

"That's excellent, Ewan. You seem to be making a good start, and Mrs Oliphant says Fred enjoys it as much as you. Your dad would have liked you to learn about boats."

"You'll remember that Dad took me on visits to the oil-rigs at Peterhead and Aberdeen; they were special days for me. Dad always explained the contraptions on the decks, and how everything was built to survive the North Sea weather. We visited the fish-markets to see the trawlers off-load their catches, but I didn't like the smell. Dad often said my drawings of the ships in the harbour were spot-on, and that I should design my own boat. So, I think I should be a ship designer. Dad said I would make a good one. There you are. That's what I want, and I'll make Mum and Dad proud."

"It's good that you have ambition, and I know your school reports have been excellent. Let's have a chat with your headmaster to see what we should plan." Aunt Tilda was forever interfering in family business, and Ewan's mother would always raise her eyebrows on her overbearing opinions. Ewan decided he didn't want her anywhere near his future plans. He gave Uncle Bert a sideways glance, shook his head, and made a hidden thumbs-down, trying to semaphore with his eyebrows that she would sink any ship she got near.

CHAPTER 4

Once again, they sat round the kitchen table. Uncle Frank was in the middle of his supper, the normal Friday's fish and chips. Aunt Bessie was fussing about the table, continually wiping imaginary marks from the spotless tablecloth. Her husband was a bit of a messy eater, which gave her something to do. Ewan always guessed that her fussing was a cover for saying or doing something uncomfortable, then out it came.

"Ewan, we would like you to move in with us permanently. Your change from primary to secondary will give you a new start, and we want to make sure you can settle in there. With our bungalow at the far end of the same street and the school only two hundred yards away, it'll be convenient for you." She failed to mention that it would be more convenient for them. He had become used to being in the home he grew up in with all its good memories. Could he survive Aunt Bessie's compulsive cleaning?

"We talked with Mrs Oliphant, and it seems that Fred will have to stay with his current school until they find a suitable place."

"A suitable place where?"

"There are special schools that can help him."

"He doesn't need any help. I'll look after him. I don't have any close friends except for Fred. He needs me. Why can't you understand?"

"Ewan, you are shouting."

"Why not? You're not listening to me. No one seems to. I was angry after the accident, and Fred kept me sane. I'm not dumping him now because it's convenient for everyone else. Fred goes with me, or I don't go, period."

Ewan sat stiffly at the supper table with a red face and breathing deeply. They hadn't reckoned on him being so aggressive and protective, but they forgot about Fred; Ewan didn't. They were beginning to understand what made Ewan tick, what made him stubborn, and what led to his aggression. Uncle Frank put down his knife and fork. He had kept quiet up till now.

"Right, Ewan. You've made your point, and I tend to agree with you. I know you have been very angry since the accident, so we've tried to give you space and security. We should have asked for your opinion first," giving Bessie a sideways look as he spoke. "We will talk it through with Mrs Oliphant. I know she thinks highly of you and all you do for Fred. If she's happy, we'll set up a meeting with the head teacher." The truth was that Mrs Oliphant was eternally grateful to Ewan. She just accepted that Ewan's protective stance of Fred was deeper than any outsider could imagine. They had been through a lot together. There was one time while she was making the inevitable pot of tea and warming some scones, that she overheard Fred talking to Ewan.

"Ewan, do you think I'm ugly like the girls say I am?"

"You're not ugly. In fact, you're very good looking, and if you brushed your hair, some of them might begin to like

16

you. Daniel likes you, and he's a good judge of character, albeit in doggy terms."

"But I don't like them. They giggle at nothing and call me names. I prefer Daniel. He listens to me all the time and gives me his paw."

"The girls are jealous because they know you can always beat them at question time in class. Do you like me?"

"Never thought about it," Fred replied matter-of-factly. "Does it matter? Sometimes I see you smiling at me, and I don't know why."

"It's difficult for me to explain. You are quite direct and honest and tell me exactly what you think, even if it's an embarrassing truth. That makes me smile. Sometimes people don't want to hear the truth, but I do, so don't stop being you." Mrs Oliphant knew Fred's inevitable direct questions to Ewan were based on a sublime honesty they enjoyed.

The secondary school took some persuading, but a meeting was set up to discuss Fred's suitability. Ewan convinced Fred that the meeting was to see if they were far enough on in their studies to fit neatly into the classes.

The four of them waited in the school admin office. Mrs Oliphant had been reluctant to expose Fred to cross-examination, but Aunt Bessie thought Fred's ability to answer direct questions was just what was needed. While they were whispering about what to say about the boys' backgrounds, Fred spoke to Ewan in a fairly loud voice.

"Ewan, you told me I had to be here to tell them what I think of your physics and maths ability. Have you completed that latest trigonometry calculation, as they may ask me?"

"Sure have, Fred, and the sine comes out exactly as you

had it. But all you need to tell them is that you are smarter than me. You don't have to explain the workings. Don't mention sports unless they ask. And if they do, say you are a keen cyclist and leave it at that. Uh, oh. Here they come."

Introductions over, the headmaster in his black gown, accompanied by his red-haired assistant, took positions on the opposite side of the table. On the wall above the headmaster was a painting of a three-masted sloop passing into the bay, with the Lochain Hills in the background. It caught Fred's attention, and before the headmaster could get a word in, Fred gave full details of the craft down to the last binnacle; it was a boat that had been moored in his dad's marina for as long as he could remember. The headmaster smiled, nodded appreciatively, and stood up.

"I don't need to hear any more. That was my grandfather's yacht, and I am obviously in good company. We look forward to you both starting next term. Let us know if you have any concerns, and we can discuss them separately." They all trooped out with Fred asking them why they were smiling. No one answered. Fred would move schools with Ewan.

The school routine suited Ewan and Fred, though at one point, the routine looked threatened. One of the bigger boys, a class above, continually gave Fred verbals and tried to put him down at every opportunity, calling him names, and forever asking why he didn't play football. They were always doing it, but Ewan just told Fred to ignore the pin-brain, loudly enough for the bully to hear him and close enough to intervene if necessary, but the bully was all mouth.

It was at a parents' evening where Aunt Bessie and Mrs

Oliphant were discussing progress with the form teachers. Ewan and Fred were out of sight behind the bike sheds. Fred was trying to get the chain of his bike back on and getting dirty hands in the process.

"Well, if it isn't our retarded turd, with hands and face to match." The bully started on Fred again. "Why don't you just shut up telling us about what you're thinking. We don't want to hear the crap that spouts out of your mouth, or should I say, arse. You're as far back as retards can go."

At that, Ewan flipped. In a welter of blows and kicks, he released all his pent-up anger. He felled the bully, giving him a black eye, and smacked the bully's mate as he tried to kick Ewan. "You ever say anything like that again, any of you, and you'll wish you had never been born. Gang up on me, or Fred, and I'll make your life outside school hell. You might look over your shoulder a bit more often on dark nights. And another thing, if I see or hear any of you make fun of Fred again, watch out. He's my best friend." The bullies retreated into the playing field with Ewan's eyes fixed to their backs. He meant it and couldn't believe where he found the courage. "Fred, are you all right?"

"What was that about? All I wanted to do was fix my chain. Why are they so aggressive?"

"They probably have a problem at home and want to take it out on someone, but it won't be you, believe me. Let's fix that chain." They found Aunt Bessie and Mrs Oliphant still chatting to some teachers. Ewan's face was flushed; his brain was doing somersaults, and his hands were still clenched, with blood where his fingernails had bitten into his palms. He didn't know what gave him the courage, but he felt better.

"What have you two been up to? Ewan, your face is all red, and Fred looks covered in oil."

"We had a problem with Fred and his bike-chain, but all's well now."

Ewan's approach to life after the loss of his parents was to keep everyone at arm's length, except for Fred. Ewan's thoughts were his own and were going to remain locked up, but Fred was a challenge. They often stood together in the playground, but one day, just before a maths class, Fred put a hand on Ewan's shoulder.

"Look, I've been told I'm different." Taken aback, as this was the first time Fred had spoken outwardly about himself, Ewan took a deep breath. He had been told about the autism scale, but it hadn't really registered with him. He had become used to its signs, and couldn't care less what people thought, but he cared what Fred thought.

"I've been told to make allowances for you, but that's about it."

"I belong to Asperger's."

"Is that a football team or a tennis club?"

"No, dummy. It means I've difficulty forming relationships, so the doctor said."

"But what does he know about it? What relationships? We get on okay, don't we?

"I suppose so, but he said I need routine."

"Well, we get up in the morning, go to school, have a bike ride, go down to the harbour, have tea, and go to bed. What else does he want you to do?"

"Mum said following the same timetable is good for me and that's it."

"Well, I'm not changing, and I need routine as well. I

daren't upset Aunt Bessie's cleaning rota. We'll stay as we are right now, if that's okay with you."

"Yup, and the doctor said I've other strengths that make up for being methodical."

"I don't know what you're talking about, but it all sounds kind of weird. What other strengths?"

"I've a photographic memory, and I can do sums in my head."

"I agree you've a way with numbers, but I've not seen you photograph anything. I've only known you as Fred, and we get on okay, and we keep ourselves to ourselves. So, nothing needs to change. I want to keep myself to myself, just like you. Since I lost Mum and Dad, I've wanted to stay private."

"I only have a mother; my dad's always away at the marina," Fred said matter-of-factly, with no hint of seeking sympathy. "So, we must be about the same." Ewan nodded and looked Fred in the eye but could read nothing from his expression.

The routine they established served them both well. They cycled everywhere, regardless of the weather. What they lacked in day-to-day conversation was filled by Fred's encyclopaedic knowledge. It came in handy when they were doing homework, and Fred would correct the result as a matter of duty but show no emotion, even when Ewan got his answers hopelessly wrong. Every so often, Ewan would get a hug from Fred for no apparent reason in front of his mother. Mrs Oliphant shrugged her shoulders when Ewan looked in her direction after an episode in the kitchen. Ewan challenged Fred out of earshot of Mrs Oliphant.

"What was that for?"

"I read that people do that to acknowledge companionship. Do you want me to stop?"

"No, no. Just do what makes you comfortable. It should pull you down the spectrum a little," but the comment was lost on Fred.

CHAPTER 5

Ewan sat in his first secondary school class unknown by anyone except Fred, and he was happy to remain private. Fred was in a world of his own. His place on the autistic spectrum had been explained to Ewan by the form teacher, that it was nothing to worry about, and that Fred was a genius at maths. Ewan already knew that. Fred always spoke as if reciting poetry or speaking to a rather dumb audience. Sometimes he circled the playground and made repetitive gestures with his hands as if talking to a companion. Most boys gave him a wide berth as if he were tainted or had a disease. Ewan kept Fred close company, without having to talk. They didn't need to talk.

When they joined the secondary school, Ewan was taken aside, "for a little talk", his mother had said. Ewan hated "little talks"; they always ended badly.

"You've been with Fred in nursery school and primary and got along well, haven't you?"

"Yup. He's not very happy, but I've become used to it."

"Fine. At this new secondary school, Fred might find it a bit intimidating; you know – scary, with new people and new surroundings. So be gentle with him. He will have to find a new routine that keeps him safe. Make allowances if he seems unhappy. Don't let anyone force him to play ball or climb trees and tell me if you see something you don't like."

"Well, I'll be new too. I'm even going to take up squash. The sport's teacher thought it would be good way for me to release any tension, or something like that. I had a session last week and it was fun. I've even been given my own racquet. Someone had donated it when they left. It's a Dunlop. Fred watched me play and told me what I was doing wrong, as if he knew. Anyway, we'll stick together, don't worry, and I won't let Fred near my racquet."

In the years growing up together, Ewan and Fred developed a relationship, both inside and outside school. Fred's mum continuously thanked Ewan, despite Ewan trying to explain that Fred was his lifesaver and that they were like two peas in a pod. Both kept their own counsel. Fred excelled at all subjects except PT, and his sharp brain pulled Ewan in his wake.

CHAPTER 6

Ewan's dad had worked in the oil industry, or to be more precise, in the rig business. The nearby Nigg basin was the temporary home for lots of rigs either preparing to face the roiling North Sea, or recovering from a long bout stuck to its bed in one of the choppiest seas in the World. They were giants of steel, built as if some large knitting needles had run amok. Pipes and tubes fought with staircases as part of some fiendish snakes and ladders game. His dad had preferred this work compared to his previous long stint in the trawler industry, which was both dangerous and precarious, not helped by a vicious Cod War. It also gave Ewan experience of a new world, with the rig divers explaining how they survived. As a present for his first teenage birthday, his uncle arranged for him to attend a session in the dunker with the divers.

It was intimidating as Ewan stepped into the huge hall with its deep swimming pool. At the far end, half in the water, was, he was told, the bright orange fuselage of a helicopter. A bunch of orange-suited men were entering the aircraft's door, and Ewan saw others get into the water. There was lots of shouting, with the echoes building up a sense of urgency. As the last man was strapped into his seat, a klaxon sounded, and the contraption turned over and sank to the bottom. Ewan had to stop holding his breath as the seconds passed, then an orange suit surfaced, followed by lots more. A supervisor was shouting out a count as each head bobbed, until a cry of "All Clear" echoed round the hall. As the men made it to the deck, shouts of relief grew louder and louder. For them, the ordeal was over, and Ewan could sense their feeling of achievement. One of the guys who passed shrugged his shoulders and said, "It's not the *Titanic*, we all came back."

Ewan's uncle introduced him to the supervising divers after the session, and they patiently explained the whys and wherefores that made the dunker so critical to the men's lives. The regular commuting by helicopter to the rigs had elements of danger that might involve ditching, so practice was essential. Uncle Frank sidled over to Ewan with a wetsuit.

"Here, try this on."

"What? I can't get into that. It'll swallow me."

"Look, this is the chance of a lifetime, and I guarantee you'll be amazed at how you feel afterwards. I was when I had a go."

Ewan struggled to get his legs and arms into the right holes with an audience of laughing divers. It was far too big and all rubbery, but with it finally on, he was led gingerly to the steps. As he let go of the step rail, he felt himself start to float, and he enjoyed the sensation. The air built up under his chin and left at the rear of his neck with a ripping, farting noise. Some of the divers were creasing themselves, and Ewan's face was redder than the suit. But the water seemed friendly, and the rubber smell meant business. Slowly, the buoyancy gave him confidence, and his grin started. This rubber scuba-gear made him feel invincible; a spark was lit.

Getting out of the suit was another giggling moment, with so many helping hands involved. Out of the suit, he looked like he had peed his pants, and despite him saying there must be a leak, they all just nodded and smirked. They said he looked the part and if he was confident in the water, he would be welcome to join their exclusive band. Ewan's uncle nodded and so did Ewan. They offered him membership of their own divers' club, which proved to be a privilege that made him the envy of his classmates. He left them on a high with many calls for him to return on their next practice. Ewan couldn't say anything and just kept nodding and grinning.

The head diver, a close friend of Uncle Frank, arranged for Ewan to join the scuba-diving club; Ewan was hooked. He enjoyed the release of tension that came from the underwater world. He was a star pupil and excelled at their practices. Many of the members were from the 'dunker world', and Ewan would listen to all their wise words, and laugh at their crude jokes. On his fourteenth birthday, he qualified for his Professional Association of Diving Instructors Open Water certificate, with a session in the dunker to celebrate. They cheered as he broke the surface.

Some of the divers were volunteers at the local lifeboat station, and he and Fred would spend hours learning about the tasks involved, and when the maroons went off, they raced to the pier-head to witness the launches. They became joint mascots and were provided with cut-down oilskins. It was a heady time for them both but, as ever, Fred never showed any evident enjoyment. Uncle Bert, his dad's younger brother, took a shine to Ewan's achievements and encouraged him to get as many boat qualifications as he could. He had left the trawler business to set up a marina and diving school in Paradise Harbour, a Scottish enclave in Bermuda. He was always at loggerheads with Fred's dad as they compared marina status. He came back regularly and was forever boasting about his success. Ewan saw the inevitable pictures with their blue skies and expensive boats, and when Uncle Bert hinted at summertime employment, all expenses paid, Ewan was all for it. Strangely, Uncle Bert had only taken an interest in him after the accident, so an element of guilt may have been behind the offer. Getting the qualifications had been an exciting priority, and he didn't care where any guilt lay.

CHAPTER 7

Out of the shelter of Nigg Bay in the breezy Moray Firth, life onboard a trawler was dangerous, poorly rewarded, and a dead end. Fred's dad had quit the trawler game early, and, starting small, took a share in a boatyard and marina just north of Invergordon. He was welding broken machinery, patching holes, straightening rudders, and cleaning bottoms. The marina also started small, but the "yachties", with their gin palaces and ocean-going yachts, were willing to spend on refurbishments and repairs at eye-watering prices set by Fred's dad. His charge for bottom scraping was obscene.

Fred and Ewan spent their weekends learning about boats and earning pocket money scraping barnacles off the bottoms. Extra services of de-salting decks and rigging paid handsomely. Fred's natural fixation with detail and repetition stood them in good stead. The powerful jet hoses were a source of fun for Ewan and fascination for Fred, who would use the spray to highlight the flow down the hulls and over the decks. The running commentary about drag and fluid dynamics lodged somewhere to pop up later. What did impress anyone listening in was Fred waxing lyrical about the shape of North Sea trawlers' bows, then comparing them with the form of the ocean-going yachts.

Ewan caught the bug and designing new ships in Fred's bedroom kept them both content and helped Fred's mother get a welcome break. Ewan marvelled at Fred's self-taught expertise in shipping design, which brushed onto Ewan unheralded.

It was Ewan's fifteenth birthday, and Fred arrived at his house out of breath, with an unusual display of unbridled enthusiasm.

"You've got to come."

"Where?"

"The marina. A flying boat has arrived."

They pedalled like mad down the cliff brae and just as they turned into Crab Lane, Ewan spotted the strange form standing on the slipway.

"It's a Buccaneer LA, four, two hundred," Fred quoted confidently. "It has four seats and is powered by a Lycoming one-eighty horsepower engine. It's owned by the chap with the forty-foot catamaran that we cleaned last week; the one that gave us a forty-quid tip."

"Will we get to see inside it?"

"Dad says the chap wants the bottom of the floats scraped and has offered us the job. Are we on?"

Ewan had seldom seen Fred so animated. "You bet, but let's walk up slowly and in a dignified way as professional bottom-scrapers."

The owner, a lanky individual wearing an oversized base-ball cap back to front and dressed in a boiler suit with lots of badges, was on a stepladder pouring what looked like oil into the engine. "Bottom-scrapers at your service," Ewan said in his gruffest, no-nonsense voice.

"Well, well, if it's not the best bottom-scrapers in the

marina. What do you charge? Mind you, you have to use the best de-fouling fluid and not as strong as for the boats. This is my precious piece of aircraft history, and they don't make them like this anymore."

"A flight round the bay would be ample payment, and we'll clean the aircraft to get rid of the salt-spray," was Ewan's on-the-spot reply as he nudged Fred into silence.

"Okay, you're on. I need it done tomorrow, and as that's Saturday, I'll get you airborne on Sunday if the weather and chop is suitable." They shook hands formally, with Ewan grinning from ear to ear, and Fred fixated on the hull shape where the step change happens just behind the passenger cabin. The pusher propeller on top and the large floats made it look clumsy compared with the aircraft pictures they were used to, but the possibility of flying held an excitement that seemed to trigger something in Fred.

Ewan was desperate to get started, so they agreed to meet at eight o'clock on Saturday morning. They pedalled back slowly, with Fred still reciting the aircraft's specification. As they arrived at Fred's house, his mum was in the garden.

"Fred and I are going to clean the flying boat tomorrow, starting early. Can you make sure Fred is ready? Then we are going flying in it on Sunday."

"I'm not sure Fred would be happy to fly."

"I've convinced Fred it's part of his learning curve about fluid dynamics and hull performance, and he says he'll treat it as an academic exercise. I don't think 'happy' comes into it."

"Well, don't blame me if he backs out."

They had the hull and floats cleaned by lunchtime, and just as they started to wash and leather-off the wings, the owner passed by and Fred bombarded him with questions on hull shape, floats, and hull step. He was very patient with Fred and responded technically until Ewan had to intervene to let the chap go, though he was smiling at Fred. Fred had just kept nodding to all the responses. The renewed promise of a flight with a take-off at ten kept Ewan on cloud nine, and Fred on his back on the slipway examining the floats minutely.

Sunday saw Nigg Bay at its Sunday best: a mill pond with perfect conditions for a flight. The rigs in their uncompromising orange stood on their stalky legs protecting the anchorage. The hills in the background had a purple hue, and the aircraft gleamed in the bright morning sun. Fred was already inspecting the aircraft minutely, just as he had done yesterday. A circuit closed somewhere and released Fred from his normal dispassionate approach. The preparations and departure went in a blur, with the lifejacket straps adding a rubber smell that would cling to them for days, and the headsets made them look like they were wearing earmuffs.

"Right, you guys, can you hear me?" They both nodded vigorously. "You can talk into the mouthpiece, and we'll hear each other." Their voices came alive, and Ewan felt a tingle run through him; he couldn't believe this was real. "We'll climb to two thousand feet, and we'll follow the coast up the Cromarty Firth then go west to the Dornoch Firth Islands. There's a place just beyond Tain I want you to see; it's a landmark for me. Then we'll follow the A9 road back to Invergordon, if that's okay?"

"Sure. This is all new to Fred and me. It's fantastic and a good bottom-scraping payment." The bouncy take-off was accompanied by the noise of water on the hull, the roar of the engine at full revs, and Fred in a blissful cocoon staring at the instruments. The pilot kept up a running commentary through the headphones, including answering Fred's continuous stream of questions, questions that showed the fruits of his previous night's study of aerodynamics and hull-water behaviour. The pilot and Ewan were both impressed how quickly Fred dissected the art of flying from the science. It was a fantastic adventure for both of them, even getting some emotional reaction from Fred and possibly a key to stimulate his feelings. The pilot pointed out the blue water of the Cromarty Firth with the boats below as tiny specks. The sun glistened on the water. Seeing the islands from the air that Ewan had only seen as humps from the shore added a view he couldn't believe. The pilot banked the aircraft steeply after they crossed the islands, which brought whoops from Ewan and wide eyes from Fred.

" Look just below us. Can you see that huge building with the tall chimney?" They both nodded." That's the Glenmorangie distillery, which makes the best whisky in Scotland. I get my supplies there. When you grow up, just remember when you see one of their bottles in a bar. Right, let's follow the road back."

The arrival was just as exciting as they approached the water. With a bump, they were gliding on its surface, and relief, tinged with regret, covered both of them. It had been the trip of a lifetime.

Fred and Ewan waved their goodbyes as they cycled away. Mrs Oliphant was in the kitchen when they arrived back. "Well, how was it?"

"Amazing! Can't believe we actually went up in the air from the water. We saw all sorts of things including the Glenmorangie Distillery."

"Really?"

"Yes, because it has its name printed in big letters on the roof. The pilot said he went lower so we could read it, and it has a huge chimney. Is that the whisky Uncle Frank drinks?"

"Och, I don't know about that, but it's well known. Now, you'd better have some tea and scones." As they sat at the kitchen table, Mrs Oliphant had to relive the flight in painful detail from Fred. Ewan was convinced change was in the air and enjoyed the pun as he explained how he and Fred might collaborate in building a model flying boat. The future looked promising.

CHAPTER 8

Just as all seemed well, Fred's dad caught a severe cold, and both boys were asked to do more at the boatyard to help out. Some evenings and most weekends were spent working to keep up with the jobs, and Fred's dad failed to get better and was transferred to the local hospital. Fred seemed unable to understand what was happening, and his mother didn't let him visit in case something went wrong. And something did go wrong. Pneumonia took hold, and his dad succumbed before Fred was able to visit. The funeral was sad for Ewan, the more so because Fred seemed incapable of displaying any emotion, though Daniel seemed to sense something and stayed very close to Fred.

At the crematorium, Ewan kept a careful eye on Fred, but Fred seemed in a world of his own, just repeating every so often that he needed to get back to feed Daniel. Overall, there was nothing that Ewan could do, except give Mrs Oliphant time without having to look after Fred.

CHAPTER 9

Ewan's grades exceeded his aunt's expectations, and they had long chats about university. Fred's enthusiasm about boats and, more especially, his detailed knowledge of fluid dynamics had triggered a spark in Ewan's ambition. He wanted to design and build boats, as he'd agreed with his dad.

Part of the push came from Ewan's Uncle Frank. When Frank's trawler days were over, he became a rig inspector. To Ewan, the rigs were a mass of steel tubes and metal walkways, all leading to nowhere. But with his uncle as a guide, Ewan began to understand which bit did what. They took photos together, with Ewan making drawings, and Uncle Frank labelling the various parts. Ewan learned the secret of the massive legs and what they stored. Fred did the usual delving, and both became quasi experts on the anatomy of a rig, leading to the technical prize at school for the best project. Fred had difficulty reacting to the fulsome praise of the teachers. The future looked brighter than either could imagine.

CHAPTER 10

They both heard the postman crunch up the drive. The letter plopped on the mat, and Ewan and Aunt Bessie looked at one another.

"Go on, open it. It looks quite official and has Southampton University's coat of arms on the back."

"Okay, but if it's a rejection notice, I'll look at that MacDonald's job in town." But as Ewan read the letter, his smile, a much missed feature these last seven years, broke across his face. "Fluid Dynamics starting in September with a scholarship to cover fees and boarding. 2019 is going to be a good year. That letter the headmaster wrote definitely did the trick."

She gave him a hug. "Well done; you deserve it. Forget McDonald's. Your Uncle Frank will be pleased. You'll have the summer to do your pre-term paper, which you told George would be about rigs. He'll give you plenty of access to the chaps at Marine Blue; they've been in the rig-design business for years. They'll be able to show you models and let you see their computer drawings.

"Fred has already shown me some of his workings, though I don't understand them. I'm going to get Uncle Frank to go through it with me."

"It means you can arrive at uni all prepared with a convincing first paper to prove you mean business."

"What shall I say to Fred because he's promised to help with the rig research? I know he doesn't show much emotion, but do you think he'll sense I'm using him then deserting him?"

"Fred lives in his own world, and he's happy being there. Just let him know you'll need his expertise when you're at uni. He's probably going to work for George in the design office informally, and his technical brain will get plenty of use. Be normal with him. Use the time till September to make Fred wanted. Let him feel part of your uni prep, and he'll probably prepare you better than any crammer would."

CHAPTER 11

The departure for uni was going to be a road trip from Invergordon to Aberdeen via all the relatives in between. Then it would be train from Aberdeen to Southampton. An early problem was Aunt Bessie's idea of what he should take on the journey, covering every imaginable emergency. The bathroom scales couldn't cope with the first trial bag. Wearing multi-layers en route was her suggestion. Ewan tried but just looked like the Michelin Man, and he became very hot as well. Many items went back into the drawers for "safe-keeping" till his next home visit. Ewan had budgeted in his spreadsheet for three return train journeys in the year. Any more and he would have to look for weekend work near the uni. The local area boasted lots of marinas, and he expected the world was always short of bottom-scrapers.

Uncle Frank was a stickler for punctuality. Loading the car had been tricky. It seemed that Frank and Bessie were going to spend some time in Aberdeen with his grandparents, which meant that the small boot was already full. Aunt Bessie was always prepared for the next apocalypse, and the car groaned under the weight of her "just in case" items. Ewan noticed a tent and primus stove hiding in a corner of the boot. Maybe they always travelled expecting the worst.

With the boot already full, Ewan shared the back seat with his bulging duffel bag and back-pack, and Aunt Bessie's over-generous picnic. Two apple pies fought with flasks of tea, milk, and soup, and enough sandwiches to feed any strays on the way. This was going to be their lunch. Aunt Bessie had declared there would be no fast food stops, and she sat in the front to control the proceedings. Ewan tried to relax and hoped the stops would not embarrass him. It was distant cousins that had never showed any interest, with associated uncles and aunts that he had only seen at the funeral, a very long time ago. It seemed this was to be Aunt Bessie's triumphal march.

As Ewan stood by the car, he received a forced hug from Fred, courtesy of his mum. Ewan returned the hug and didn't want to let go. They had been through so much together but had rarely shown affection either way. Ewan felt Fred's warmth and wanted to say he loved him, but it didn't come out. "Fred, thanks for all your help. Remember I'm relying on you to check my homework." He was sorry to be leaving his best friend behind, and his eyes welled up. Even if he had told Fred how he felt, Fred would probably not have recognised the emotion or what it meant.

"You have to email me as soon as you get there to set up our distant learning exchange. I'll let you see my workings on the new floatplane, not boat plane. I've also corrected some of the calculations on your rig design, which I'll send to you. You forgot to include hydrostatic loads from swell as opposed to calm." It was typical Fred. No emotion and never any sense of bragging, just a matter-of-fact statement. Ewan would miss Fred's honesty.

"Fred, I'm relying on you as never before. I'll probably

be out of my depth, and that is a good metaphor. I will need you to rescue me." Mrs Oliphant gave Ewan a long hug and whispered that she would look after Fred just as Ewan had. Her tears wet Ewan's cheek; a memory parked away.

They set off from Invergordon exactly at seven with the sun peeking over Lochain Hill; Ewan's view from the back was limited, but he could see Fred walking away with his mum and Daniel. His tears flowed privately as he stared at the retreating figures. He knew he was losing something special, and it hurt. And he loved Daniel just as much.

Aunt Bessie didn't believe in Satnav. Her well-worn road atlas was her bible. Uncle Frank new better than to argue. They had done the route many times before, so the only comments made were Bessie's opinion on all the drivers they passed. Her language was flowery, using animal descriptions where most people would use swear words. Ewan was going to offer some of his own, but a glance from Frank warned him off. They stopped at Tarlair on the Aberdeenshire coast for their picnic lunch. It boasted a cliff-top view over an almost blue sea with some seahorses fighting in the wind. Ewan mused that there was always wind from the North Sea, and the sea temperature was a test of standing on tiptoe while pretending to be enjoying the waves as they broke on the beach. Aunt Bessie found a sheltered spot behind a huge block of concrete, a relic from an old World War Two defensive fortification. The setting left much to be desired for a lunchtime picnic. The tea was still piping hot, but Ewan had to trouser a couple of sandwiches to avoid upsetting Aunt Bessie, who couldn't appreciate that Ewan's appetite and tum were feeling the effect of the day's excitement. The next three stops were to meet the distant relatives, ones whom Aunt Bessie chose to describe as on the rich side of mean. They had money but never offered to pay. She had said as much at the funeral, and in their hearing.

The arrival at his grandparents' house on the outskirts of Aberdeen was a welcome relief from being polite to those remote relatives. He hadn't recognised any of them from the funeral. Their willingness to conjure up some semblance of family feeling left him cold. Aunt Bessie had emphasised that none of them came forward to help with Ewan's future. Ewan wondered where they were when the bad things happened.

CHAPTER 12

The huge girdered rail station at Aberdeen echoed with the metal shuffling of trains and waggons. The forecourt was crowded. People jostled one another, while some stared at the departure boards as if in a trance. Ewan was quick to spot his platform and decided not to prolong the farewells.

Grandma and Grampa were in tears. They probably saw it as Ewan off to uni and not coming back. Uncle Frank and Aunt Bessie, as surrogate parents, were stoic in their expressions, but their lips were quivering. Perhaps they thought they wouldn't see their investment in his growing up mature, despite Ewan's assurances that he would give it his all.

"Aunt Bessie and Uncle Frank. What can I say? I know I wasn't the best ten-year-old in the world, but I appreciate all you've done for me. Now it's payback time. I hope to make you proud, and Mum and Dad." Ewan hugged them both. There were no words for Grandma and Grampa. Just more heartfelt hugs. Ewan was determined to smile for them, even though his stomach was doing cartwheels. He made it through the ticket barrier, laden with his huge duffel bag, haversack, and bag of goodies from Grandma. He used his spare arm to wave goodbye and trudged along the curving platform towards the front of the train, until his family were out of sight, and he was on his own. His sense of relief to be on this life-changing journey was tinged with the fear of the unknown. Yesterday had been a whirlwind tour of his so-called next-of-kin: a continual stream of cups of tea and lots of difficult-to-swallow scones. He could now relax.

With his bag squeezed into the overhead rack, he stuck his haversack between his legs with the handle of his squash racquet sticking out like a joystick. The image reminded him of the flight in the Buccaneer amphibian a lifetime ago.

The carriage soon filled up and, as the train started off with a couple of hesitations, everything was shaken into place. He had his own space, just, but the two kids opposite him were excited and hyperactive. The mother looked frazzled and lacked the element of control that could have stopped the continual fighting. It was going to be some journey in this new world, but the novelty of departing on the next stage of his life was ample compensation.

The sound of the electric motors changing gears and the clattering of the points were welcome sounds. He began to relax and think; memories flooded in, and he nodded off.

An announcement that they were entering Edinburgh Waverly station brought Ewan back to reality. There were still many more train hours ahead. He opened his laptop to see what Fred had been up to. He skimmed through pages. It had only been a suggestion that they design a better Buccaneer floatplane, but Fred took the idea to heart. He did reams of research, from the whale-like surface of the hull to electric motors of the powertrain. Fred could always think out of the box, and this he did with a vengeance.

Ewan marvelled at the images that continued to pop up as he looked at Fred's handiwork. He had pinched the wings and tailplane design from the Russian Ekranoplan aircraft, the Monster of the Caspian Sea, which Fred stated was a ground effect vehicle of gigantic proportions. There was no comparison between the ramp at the marina in Invergordon and the ramp at the Caspian base; they were leagues apart, but to Fred it was only a simple matter of scale. Fred's enthusiasm was infectious, and Ewan started to see fluid dynamics in a different light. Looking through the joining notes for the university course, aerodynamics was a large part and, combined with water dynamics, creating a modern amphibian would be a fantastic goal. The blurb indicated that the course wanted innovative thinking. Maybe Fred would be his off-campus research fellow to make this dream come true. Unconsciously, he started to daydream again.

Being brought up among boats, oil rigs, and marinas, Ewan wondered if his enthusiasm for the water was based on the natural education that Invergordon nurtured. Even the climate was benign compared with the rest of Scotland. It hadn't been idyllic by any means, but the mechanics of the industry beat farming and sheep-rearing hands down. He remembered the harbour wall as a magnet; there was always something sailing in or out, and the orange lifeboat had a fascination better than any fire-engine. Was his journey to uni down to planning or serendipity? From now on, he was determined to make his own luck.

His mind turned to leaving Fred. He had lost something. Was it love of a kind? Their relationship had been brotherly, but a bit more. There was no physicality, apart from Fred's occasional hugs, which stemmed from encounters that left

Ewan perplexed. Fred was a fine physical specimen, very handsome, blond blue-eyed, and attractive with a magnetic innocence but no smile. When Ewan was the recipient of a hug, the meaning was never clear nor what triggered it. Ewan would have liked to respond, but the action was always over in a trice. The flash of eye-to-eye contact was brilliant, but gave Ewan too little time to respond with the warmth he wanted to show. It was Ewan's biggest regret that he felt he had failed to show his love for Fred in a way that Fred would understand. In the reality of the moving train and the noisy kids in the carriage, Ewan felt very alone.

The rest of the journey was a kaleidoscope of dreams and scenes. Sometimes he would be staring into the middle distance at unknown hills and lakes spaced suitably between stations, then see his face reflected in the window – a reality check. The kids had worn each other out and had fallen asleep. Ewan followed suit. His dreams fought one another, with some memories before the accident being replaced by the Buccaneer flight with Fred's voice invading all. But each time he thought he had a hold on his mind, the scene with the judge in court always seemed to come to the fore. It was a memory he could do without.

The arrival at Euston station was a frantic episode. The carriage erupted as the kids found their strength and voices. Ewan tried to help their mother, and, eventually, they all decanted onto the station platform. Ewan was grateful to be on his own again. Uncle Frank had been meticulous with writing everything down, underlining the route to follow. Secretly, Grandma had slipped him some money in an envelope, with a forceful instruction to get a taxi between the stations. "I don't want you distracted by the bad parts of London. You need to get to the university, and I want you to ring me the moment you get there. Remember, the taxi fare isn't a luxury in this modern world; I want nothing to get in your way. Your mother would be proud." It was a sentiment that kept echoing in his head.

Taxi it was as he watched the meter tick the money away on the hectic melee of traffic and people towards his fictional Waterloo. It was a humbling experience to be using Grandma's money to make life easier. Study would be the payback, but the current blaze of buildings, buses, cyclists, and people all rushing somewhere overwhelmed his senses. It made Invergordon seem quite staid.

The train ride from Waterloo station to Southampton was just as busy, but everyone kept themselves to themselves. Surrounded by his luggage in the middle of the carriage, the comings and goings of the commuters was great for people-watching. By the time the train entered the terminus, Ewan had diagnosed all their problems and stress levels, imagining some wanting desperately to get back to their family and others reluctant to face the drudgery of home. By their expressions, he reflected that his life was less stressful, but he was absolutely alone, rudderless, and scared.

The taxi dumped him, baggage and all, outside the large, central building with the university's coat of arms. Avenues of buildings spread in all directions, and he was fairly certain that he glimpsed a distant sparkle that was almost certainly the Solent. He had to pinch himself that he had finally arrived without too much aggro, thanks to Grandma.

The admission process was well regimented, possibly to

take care of hillbillies like him. Form-filling was a competition to see how many different ways he could identify himself. The checklists mounted up, but the last one as he sat down in his allocated bedroom was the best. The inventory of the room consisted of one item – the only one that wasn't attached to the wall, the floor, or the ceiling – the toilet seat. Ewan wondered how many had disappeared over the years to make this so important. A repayable deposit would have been a better approach. The motherly figure who had led him to his room pointed to the WC.

"You had better check the seat before signing. We have no end of problems," she said without intending the pun. He checked its condition before signing.

"What has been the problem?"

"It's something to do with end-of-term, and a challenge between houses. You'll find out soon enough. Your other challenge is to keep your bedding safe; it's on my inventory. The laundromat is in the basement, and here is a box of soap powder that the last chap left. I clean the rooms so I know what should be here. You keep it safe for me, and I'll make sure your room smells of roses."

"I will, but probably roses might be too much. How about lily of the valley?" She laughed and nodded with a smile. He felt this was a good start, but the theft of his toilet seat would be another matter.

CHAPTER 13

He hardly slept. This was reality day. The room was so clinical. The desk folded down from the wall; the seat folded down from the desk; the bed folded up into the wall; the armchair was screwed to the floor. Even the waste-bin was nailed to the back of a cupboard, and the chalk and pin board had no visible screws or bolts. He hadn't brought any mementos, except for the photos on his laptop, so the atmosphere was what he assumed prison would be, except he had a magnificent view of the River Itchen from his third-floor perch in the Glen Eyre halls of residence. He could make out the university's water-sports centre: that would be his substitute wall picture. The boats bobbed invitingly in the far distance, with echoes of the marina back home.

He had started to get his bearings, though finding his way to the eating hall for breakfast was a challenge. He used his nose rather than be seen to be consulting the cheat-sheet. He ended up at the kitchen entrance, before doubling back to the canteen. It was all bustle and hustle, so he followed the herd, and made it to an empty table. He had arrived a week ahead of Freshers' Week, as recommended by his headmaster, who felt it better to get settled in and set off confident. Confidence wasn't his strong point, and the table filled up with strangers. They started asking him questions, so he responded between mouthfuls with answers that must have made him out as a country bumpkin. But no one laughed at him, and two of them were also early to get into the swing. He started to relax when he heard their academic journey to uni was similar to his. He felt less anxious.

The rest of the week was designed around background reading provided by the course tutor. The books were weighty tomes with little fiction and plenty of fact. Some were sources of boredom; others hinted at incompatible laws of physics. The Flat Earth Society would have been up in arms. Ewan took to studying in the morning, and sightseeing in the afternoon to become familiar with the area.

The SeaCity Museum was first, and the sight of the flying boats triggered a flashback to Fred's idea of designing a new aeroplane. Against budget and with unusual balmy autumn weather, Ewan hired a bike and cycled everywhere, criss-crossing the area to take in the old boat and train terminals, and the Supermarine Works, the birthplace of the Spitfire. Seeing the real craft that demonstrated the content of the textbooks provided a welcome antidote to the crushing boredom of the pages. In the few days he had to explore, Ewan felt he had arrived at a place that would influence his future. He took some photographs of plenty of aircraft exhibits to send to Fred, including ones of the original BOAC flying boats, and hoped it might hint at getting their aircraft design started.

CHAPTER 14

Having spent the week getting his bearings and avoiding people, the uni programme took over on the following Monday. The compulsory Freshers' Week was starting, where meeting people was inevitable. His plan was to stay in the background and keep a low profile, select a sport, and join a club allied to his studies.

The uni common room was huge. There seemed to be much on offer, with music and drama everywhere he looked. The club stands circled the periphery, and the throng ebbed and flowed as if a giant hand was swirling them in a bucket of water. Ewan found himself pressed up against a stand that advertised the Sailing Society. He felt it could be the answer to his prayers. The principal subject for his nominated degree was fluid dynamics. He was interested in hull shapes; why not learn to sail properly? Just as he approached and turned to face the booth, a guy was standing immediately in front of him holding out a bunch of leaflets. He had light hazel eyes flecked with green that shone like emeralds. Ewan was transfixed until the guy saw him staring. He caught the returning quizzical look before he had time to avert his gaze. They were about six feet apart with a crowd pressing around. Ewan turned back to see that the chap now had a huge grin on his face, and Ewan had no escape route. Ewan blushed and turned to go but felt a tap on his shoulder.

"Where are you going?

"Nowhere."

"Want to sail?"

"Y-yes," stammered Ewan, his voice trembling in embarrassment.

"Good. You've found the right place. I'm Tom Braithwaite, membership secretary. And you are?"

"I'm Ewan Begg, wet behind the ears and probably looking out of my depth."

"Don't worry, we don't throw you in at the deep end. What's your core subject?"

"Engineering centred on fluid dynamics."

"Good choice. You must be smart with numbers." Ewan detected a Yorkshire accent with a hint of something else. He was Ewan's height with blond, curly hair. The eyes were remarkable, and Ewan couldn't help focussing on them. The guy smiled broadly with brilliant white teeth. "Look. Let's sit down and take some details."

"Okay, but does it cost to join? I'm lean on finance."

"No, and there are ways round the membership fee, but more later. Have you signed up for anything else?"

"Only squash, my sport."

"Brilliant. I play. Are you any good?"

"I've no finesse, but I scuttle about."

"Are you about this evening? I have a court booked for seven, but my partner has just called off. It would be great to have a game."

"Yes, I'm free." Ewan thought his diary was light on

detail and wanted it to stay that way.

"Right, let's get the Sailing Club paperwork done, and I'll let you go."

As Ewan left the stand, he felt elated that someone had talked to him in a normal way, and he couldn't shake off the mesmeric eyes, framed by long eyelashes; women would die for them – what a thought.

CHAPTER 15

Ewan arrived early at the sports centre behind the Students' Union. The courts were state-of-the-art with glass everywhere, and the gym was stocked with the latest torture equipment. He had his Dunlop racquet, but when he checked in at reception to pay his membership, he was told it had been paid already by "our Yorkshireman" and was given a locker key. He was puzzled. All this was new to him; he felt like an intruder. Changing into his kit, he noticed that most players had the latest clothing logos; his clothing and shoes were anything but flashy. With relief, he spotted Tom arriving.

"Ewan, thanks for making it. I wasn't looking forward to practising on my own; it's pretty tedious but supposed to be good for you, they say. Are you fit?"

"I think so, but I've been told my membership and court fees have been paid. Was that you?"

"All taken care of."

"But I've got to pay my way, and it was in my budget. And the receptionist said it was paid by a Yorkshireman. They are reputed to be tight, the definition being a Scotsman with all the generosity removed. And In case you haven't noticed, I'm a Scotsman. Was that you?"

"Look, my dad's in oil, and he can't spend it fast enough, so I have to help him. I have to keep my expenses up. Every little helps. Now let's get going. I like your racquet. Do they still make them?"

"Well, I trust it, and yours looks too clean, and I don't have designer shorts, shirt, or shoes, but all-white is easier to wash. Does that stripe on your shoes make you go faster?"

"You'll see."

Entering the court, Ewan immediately felt at home. Looking forward was fine, but the glass back wall was unfamiliar. He was used to pure white walls; assessing position and length was going to be tough with such a dark background. They warmed up fairly with an even number of shots, and Ewan could see Tom had a deft touch, especially at the front, but knew that people could look good during the warm-up with play a different matter.

Tom won the toss and had an easy first game. Ewan couldn't sight the ball at the back of the court. He dreaded a whitewash. On the second game, Ewan started using his "badminton" feint to flick the ball over Tom's shoulder, and the satisfying *plop* into the back corner started to come off. It was close, but Ewan won the second. The third was played to Ewan's pattern. Sidewall hugging shots, neat lengths, lots of feints, with satisfying reverses at the front, made Tom puff, with Ewan managing to be in the right place at the right time. Tom was now swearing at the ball. Ewan smiled back. At the finish, they were both pooped, but Tom had the redder face. They both laughed.

"Well done. I thought I had you at the start."

"That bloody glass wall appeared black to me; you know, just like the colour of the bloody ball."

"I just thought you didn't know how to play."

"Well, you know now, but it was great fun."

"Winner normally shakes hands and buys the drink, but you can give me a man-hug instead to save the money." And they clinched. The hug lasted longer than Ewan expected, although something inside him wanted it to go on for ever. They separated, and all Ewan could do was to stare into those beautiful eyes; then the blush came.

"Sorry. I was staring again. It's your bloody eyes. I can't stop looking at them." They both laughed.

"I don't mind. It lets me try and see what's behind you. The showers are round the corner. You may have noticed I worked up quite a sweat."

"I tried to give the impression I didn't, but my torso is a giveaway. That first game was knackering."

The changing rooms and showers were empty and echoing. They sat down to cool off.

"Look, that thing about my dad and money. He's in South Africa, and owns an oil-servicing consultancy, and they pay him big bucks to cover their arses. He's away all over the world, so he compensates me and my sister with guilt money. It's as simple as that. We live in a big house in Cape Town with servants. My mum tries to keep us grounded, and makes sure we do chores and cooking, despite having a cook. When we're there, we have to study doubly hard to offset our leisure time, which for me is sailing. I even qualified for my inshore and offshore skipper's ticket. Okay, my dad has a state-of-the-art fifty-foot yacht, but it meant he was hard on us, and the examiners were even harder. Sarah, my older sister, is just as qualified. Getting me onto an MBA course was Dad's idea, so here I am. Sorry, I seem to have spilled most of my beans. Your turn."

"Well, I got here by keeping my head down, suppressing any thoughts of people I liked or disliked, and aimed for uni as a way out. Don't get me wrong, I had a great childhood until I was ten with hugs that always solved my problems. I was so happy. My dad was one of four brothers, all trawlermen based around the Cromarty Firth and the north coast of Aberdeenshire in Scotland. The Cod War and poaching by the Russian factory ships killed the trade, but the fishing industry's loss was the oil industry's gain. They all moved across, my dad included, and they were glad to say goodbye to the atrocious weather conditions and the lottery of missed catches. He was more at home and his enthusiasm for the rigs rubbed off on me. We had fun times. Then a looney driver killed my parents in a car accident when he thought his phone was more important than my parents' lives. I sat through the court case. He was sent down for ten years. The judge said I was given a life sentence, and he was right."

"Look, you don't have to go on."

"That's why I don't want ever to get too close to people that could leave me like that again. My best friend at school was autistic, and I couldn't tell him that I liked him, so it was emotionally draining. It made me a bit of a recluse. It still hurts. Sometimes I can't sleep. It pisses me off that I have to put up a barrier. I'm already prepared to see you disappear. That's how it works, and that's me in a nutshell. Sorry for the off-load."

"Let's cool off at my flat. It's just across from the uni. And before you ask, my dad decided I would do a foundation course in accounts before starting my degree proper; that's why I left SA and came here last year. He reckoned I'd be here for four years so, in his wisdom and wealth, he bought the flat for me, and my sister when she visits. It's no big deal, and I guess it's better than the Halls of Residence, but you can be the judge. I looked at a room when I first arrived. It reminded me of a cell, with everything immovable and stark. Dad thought so as well."

"I'm just glad to be here. My room's a bit sparse, but I don't have much baggage – physical, that is. I'll probably get care packages from Grandma, so you'll get to sample some truly Scottish delicacies. I suppose all you have is Yorkshire pudding."

"You'll see. We still have our house in Yorkshire and the caretaker bakes Yorkshire pudding perfectly. I'll get her to send us some. I don't know how well it travels. Let's go. I cycle everwhere.

"I've hired a bike."

"Turn it in. You can use my sister's until they drain the canal."

CHAPTER 16

"Tom, this wine is going to my head. I've been out of practice since Hogmanay. I think I'd better go. It's difficult enough making it across the hedge-littered campus to Hill House. Then I have to negotiate the Porters' Lodge. I don't want to be pissed when I try that. I best leave while I can walk and talk."

"Hang on. I have a huge flat here. The bed is king-size and so is the sofa. Why don't you relax and stay over?"

"I've got my first induction meeting at eleven. I can't afford to be late for that. First impressions."

"We can set two alarms to get you out of here on time, I swear."

"I wasn't planning a sleep-over. My squash kit may start to hum."

"Christ, I have more clothes all cleaned and ironed than you can shake a stick at. Although you might baulk at the designer labels."

"Look. We've known one another for less than twenty-four hours, and I would look like an imposter in your gear."

"I've invited you from my heart. I think we've clicked – and there are more South African wines for you to try.

They're from our own vineyard. I hope that doesn't sound too pretentious. My sister Sarah runs the vineyard. She would be pleased to get a Scottish view. You like the wine, don't you? Neither of us is into beer, and it makes a welcome change from pretending to be one of the lads and drinking pints."

"I must be crazy to say yes. I've never done anything like this before, and feel out of my depth and a little vulnerable. Like a fawn in a car's headlights."

"You can sleep anywhere in the flat. If needs be, I'll sleep on the sofa, but come and look at the bed; it's huge. Ewan, can I ask if you're gay?"

"Tom. Can I ask if you're straight?"

"Ewan, I'm fucking sorry. It just came out 'cos I wanted you to be."

"I am not out, and don't want to be. I need to finish this course with zero distraction. I can wank and put those thoughts aside."

"Okay. But if I said I wasn't out, and was like you, would that make a difference?"

"Only if we shared the same closet."

"Well, if you show me yours, I'll show you mine." They both grinned and laughed, staring at one another.

"Chardonnay again?"

"And I propose a toast. To our secret."

"To our secret."

"Will you stay?"

"What do you think?"

"Do you snore?"

"Do you?"

"No idea."

"I want to talk, pissed as I am, and staying in a stranger's flat. I'm not sure about you, but I have butterflies in my belly when I look into your eyes. God knows where the butterflies come from; I'm not a lepidopterist. I think I said that right. It feels good, and I want to crumple into your arms. I've never let my guard down like this before. It's as if I'm eagerly awaiting my next disappointment. In the cold light of day, reality always kicks me in the balls."

"Right, I know we've just met, but the way I feel right now, I'm in heaven, and that can't be true because my love life has been more hope over substance. Yes, outwardly I look happy and fulfilled, but it's all a façade. So, when you looked at me at the Freshers' meet, there was a little earthquake. Our eyes must have only been fixed for microseconds, but the speed of light can work wonders. That's why I cocked my head to question your look. You instantly blushed, and I knew something special had just happened. That's why I walked towards you. It's a moment imprinted on my memory. How about you?"

"I shake to think it was that obvious. Now we are here, and I am being asked to stay the night. I bet it's a bloody dream as usual, and I'll wake up to a shitty reality."

"Come here. This is reality." Tom initiated the kiss, and Ewan tingled all over from the warmth of the man-hug. It was a feeling he had never experienced before, and his brain did somersaults as he tried to capture the moment.

They collapsed onto the big bed, and both discovered one another. Ewan had never been this close to a naked warm body before, and it felt good and secure. Tom just melted into his arms, and their inhibitions disappeared as the wine had done from the bottles. At times, their hands explored one another; at others, they were locked in an embrace that gave no hiding place for their feelings. Everything was on show, and neither felt any inhibition for the strength of feeling between them. Eventually, Ewan sensed Tom had fallen asleep and could only smile at where a squash game had led. He was the winner on all counts. Then sleep took over.

CHAPTER 17

Ewan woke first and could not believe that he was still entangled with the beautiful boy that had been in his dream and didn't even have a sore head. Tom stirred and the dream became reality.

"Hello. You'll be Ewan, my squash partner from last night."

"Yup. And you'll be Tom, who gave me my best night's sleep ever. I hope I didn't embarrass you last night. I just let go of everything. You could probably tell I'm new at this. Apologies if I was too physical, but you are bloody attractive – all over. I took my lead from you. And you smell inviting; what is it?"

"Jo Malone. It's a cologne – Yorkshire oak and redcurrant. Okay, maybe I added the 'Yorkshire' bit."

"Well, it did the trick. Now, do you mind if I kiss you?"

"No. You were perfect for me. I needed the chance to break a spell that has been haunting me. We both need confirmation that this isn't a dream." The kiss lasted till the alarm broke the spell.

"Much as I want to stay like this forever, we need to get going. Remember, I have my induction meeting at eleven. We'll have to untangle, if that's the right word, and get showered. You better go first to show me the way. Why are we both still smiling like dopes?"

"I think it's something to do with what you said last night."

"What was it?"

"That if we keep smiling now that we have a joint secret, it will make everyone wonder what we've been up to, and they can think what they like 'cos our mouths are sealed as agreed."

"As agreed, so one more kiss?"

The cycle ride to the lecture hall was unabashed fun, with each grinning from ear to ear. To Ewan, it was a momentous start to the term, feeling as he did that he just might have found love or something like it. He didn't dare talk to Tom about it in case it punctured his dream.

CHAPTER 18

The first term followed a pattern that gave Ewan a feeling of security. Although it was difficult to adjust to his new-found friendship and its necessary secrecy, Tom was an anchor in more ways than one. His sailing friends welcomed Ewan and took him at face value; he was a novice and said so. They responded by taking time to educate him in the sailing disciplines, which gave him sore hands and a decent lump on his head if he didn't duck when they went about. It was all good-humoured fun. Eric was on the same academic course so could sympathise, and Claire was on a business management course and able to bring the chat down to a bearable, non-physics level. As a group, the four of them melded, and Tom made sure the sailing targets were kept in sight. Even at weekends, they took it as read that they would sail. Ewan learned fast and an in-shore ticket was to be his goal.

Tom understood Ewan's need to concentrate during the week, so made weekends special. They talked and talked, sometimes revealing more than they intended. One evening, the subject of the future reared its head.

"Ewan, can I ask you what you want to do once you graduate?"

"Not sure, but I have this idea of designing a flying boat, and Fred, my autistic best mate at school who I've talked about, is so keen to take part, I don't want to disappoint him. I owe him a lot."

"Does that mean you would stay in this area?"

"I think so. It has so much history, and it's warmer down here than frosty Scotland. What about you?"

"Well, my dad sent me here to do the six-month primer course in accounts last year and wants me to complete a degree in business management to take some pressure off his consultancy. As well as being a small yacht builder on the side, he has been into oil exploration, successfully, so now the business flows to him, as does the money. Being from Yorkshire, he has worked hard and earned the right to spend it – so he says."

"But will you have fun working for him?"

"I'm not sure, but I owe him. I had a great childhood, and we are close. But now Dad needs help with the yachting enterprise, and the money will be good. I know money isn't everything, but I can sail and drink wine. Do you want to help me?"

"What, with the wine? I'm already in training."

"No, what I meant was, could you see yourself moving to South Africa with me?"

"I think the best place to use my degree would be here in the UK aviation and sailing industry. It leads the world, and can you imagine the fun of designing a new aircraft? Fred and I had a trip in a Buccaneer float plane; I was hooked, and Fred seemed to be in his element. We both agreed to make a state-of-the-art aeroplane; the one we flew in was a bit old. I know I have zero commercial qualifications, but the magic of a new floatplane, built using the latest 3D technologies with advanced carbon structuring, could open up a new mode of transport for flightseeing and short transport trips. Does that make sense to you?"

"Okay, but you could come to South Africa during the hols and keep me company."

"I would love to, but I promised my uncle I'd help again with his marina in Bermuda. It's part of the Scottish contingent that left Inverness when the fishing industry collapsed. I also help at his diving school, and I get seconded to the inshore lifeboat. It makes a brilliant break, and it's so peaceful and slow. You ought to come with me."

"I'm tempted, but I'm torn and duty calls."

"Well, if not this year, maybe next? We'll just have to keep finding ways to be together."

CHAPTER 19

Ewan's mobile rang; it was Tom. "Can you make it over here? I need your help with a party to celebrate a friend's birthday."

"But you know I don't like parties, especially if it's your Hooray Henry alleged friends."

"Please. They are not 'alleged' friends; we all went to school together."

"They're a bunch of spongers, male and female. They drank you out of booze last time, and none of them brought anything. They think your accent is country bumpkin and know you're monied, or at least your dad is."

"Look, if it makes me happy, can't you lay your prejudices aside for once?"

"But it's not once. They take the piss. The drugs are just as bad, and they treat your room as a fornicatorium. Their lack of hygiene is a disgrace. I had to clean the floor and toilets with Dettol. I know you're a strong Yorkshireman, but I see them weave a web as they have always done, selfishly, brazenly, artfully, and unashamedly. Do you want me to go on? They show no respect. They find my Scottish accent a source of merriment, and your accent a source of spending. I hate it. I want to protect you from those bastards

– and the girls are the worst. Who pays for all those drugs? Honestly, Tom, I need to escape that clique, and you do too. I'll pop in to make an appearance but won't stay long once I'm satisfied you're okay. I can't be myself with you in front of them; you know that. I'll call in tomorrow with the usual fumigator. Hopefully, they'll have gone home before I get there. So tonight, I'll make an entrance, then leave you to the Henrys, the Taras, the Ruperts, and Jemimas."

"Ewan, you're prejudiced."

But the following morning after the previous night's disengagement, Ewan felt pity for Tom. They had done their best to appear unconnected, yet they both felt a pang of despair that they couldn't appear as a couple.

Ewan made it from the Hall of Residence to Tom's flat in ten minutes. The Sunday traffic was minimal, and the gentle patter of rain had stopped the recreational bikers. The lift smelled of wee and, as the lift doors opened, it was as if a skunk had been trapped and triggered its defence mechanism.

The flat was a complete mess. Marigolds would be the order of the day. A bleary-eyed Tom appeared from the kitchen. "Hi."

"Hi. Are there any bodies on the premises, and do I get a kiss or a hug?"

"No, they departed to the pub early, and here's a hug."

"Will we be alone, or will they return?"

"They've gone with Rupert. His parents are holding a soiree in Southsea to promote a local artist. We are invited."

"We?"

"Well, no, I am."

"You go. I'll clean up here and do paperwork for our

presentation. Sunday is a good day for contemplation, and we can pick holes in our logic."

"For fuck's sake, relax, Ewan. They are my friends, and they make merry. They lift my spirits."

"That's true: they lift your booze, and sometimes your credit card. I keep saying I want to protect you."

"I don't need protecting."

"Let me be the judge of that, Tom. I have this feeling about you. It's irrational; it's on a plane I don't recognise, and it's deep inside me. Please don't dismiss it out of hand. It may protect us both from those that could do harm. I hope that doesn't sound too profound."

Ewan looked deeply into Tom's eyes and felt the weight of the moment and something that he was beginning to recognise.

"Sorry."

"Sorry. I just feel protective of you; of us, of course. I hope that's not too soppy." The mutual smile bridged the gap.

"Can I come back to your Hall of Residence tonight so I'm on time for Monday's lecture?"

"Yes. Let's go. Make sure you pack your designer clothes. I don't have spares. And make sure you double lock the door to stop those bastards getting back in."

"Okay. Let's get our bikes and go. My duffel is already packed; I can suss you."

CHAPTER 20

The first two months passed with squash and sailing proving an ideal safety valve. The lectures followed a pattern that was a steep learning curve for Ewan, but he remained enthusiastic. Fred's continual email feed was breathtaking; the detail and research meant a great deal to Ewan. All was peaceful until …

It was Sunday evening, but the clock said two a.m., Monday morning. He was awake in an instant. Someone was trying to kick his door in. Adrenalin started to flow. Grabbing his squash racquet, he strode to the door, turned the lock as quietly as he could, then snatched the door bolt open quickly. The sight that met him was terrible. Tom stood in front of him, soaking wet, covered in mud, with red eyes and a look of terror. Ewan pulled him in, checked that the corridor was empty, closed the door and slid the bolt across.

Dripping puddles on the floor, Tom looked as if ghosts had chased him. He was shaking all over, and his stammer prevented any recognisable words. Then this normally bluff Yorkshireman collapsed into Ewan's arms. The hug was wet and cold. Tom was sobbing. Something was seriously wrong. Ewan gently lowered Tom on to the couch, grabbed a towel from the bathroom, and towelled Tom's plastered hair and wiped his mud-splattered face.

"What's up. Why are you so cold and wet? You're shaking."

"I … I cycled here as fast as I could. I took the short cut over the building site."

"Okay. But has something happened at your flat?"

"There's been a robbery."

"What. At your flat?"

"No. In Cape Town. My parents were shot, murdered, during a robbery at the house – and they killed our two Labs as well. My uncle just phoned. My sister is now at their house and is safe, but she has gone silent."

"Christ, Tom, I'm so sorry. Look, you're shivering. Let's get you into a warm shower, and I'll dig out some clean clothes for you. Your hands resemble blocks of ice. It must be below zero outside." Tom nodded. His soaking hoodie came off after a struggle. Tom tried to undo his shirt buttons, but his fingers were too numb. "Here, let me do it." Not only was Tom's shirt wet but so were his jeans and T-shirt. The building site must have had some pretty big, water-filled potholes. His shoes made a squelching noise as he stood up. "Right, T-shirt next, and I'll undo your belt buckle." The jeans were stuck to his legs. "Sit on the couch while I take off your shoes and socks." Ewan pulled at the legs, but Tom seemed to have no strength, and Ewan had to roll the jeans down from the waist; it was a strange intimate struggle.

"Do you want to take your underpants off in the shower?"

"I don't think my fingers will work."

"Okay, I'll take them off. We're best friends and that's what I'm here for." Ewan steered Tom towards the shower in the bathroom, turned the shower on and checked the temperature, then removed Tom's underpants. Tom was still shaking, and Ewan recalled Tom talking about his malaria history of getting the "shakes", coupled with being out in a sub-zero temperature: the combination was a bad omen.

"In you go. Tell me if it's too hot. There are fresh towels on the shelf opposite, and I'll get some dry clothes for you. They aren't your designer ones, but they'll fit." Tom almost gave a smile. "Shout if you need anything. I'll put your stuff on the radiator to start drying out. Kettle's going on."

Ewan had difficulty dealing with the emotion that was building up. Here was his closest friend, whom he had known for only a short time, looking scared and vulnerable, a side of Tom he had never seen. That he had come to Ewan as his first action triggered something deep inside. Ewan knew his feeling for Tom had reached a new level. It was a step change that gave him a determination to protect Tom at all costs, and forever. The word "murder" sent a chill down Ewan.

Using the hairdryer to warm Tom up, and, with fresh underwear, he put him to bed. There would be plenty time to get Tom's story. For now, he needed security and rest. Ewan sat on the bed trying to give warmth to Tom's shaking shoulders. The day passed fitfully with Tom awakening now and then from some bad dream. He wouldn't eat anything despite Ewan's encouragement. The shivering continued.

In the end, Ewan got under the duvet and tried to impart as much body heat by hugging. Throughout most of the night, Ewan tried to keep hold of Tom to stop the shaking. Eventually, Tom seemed to calm down, and his breathing sounded more relaxed. But it was a disturbed sleep with Tom crying at times. It revived bad memories for Ewan that he had locked away a long time ago.

Ewan was up and dressed early, while Tom appeared to have fallen into a deep sleep. It was going to be a momentous day, and Tom would need all the help and comfort Ewan could muster.

Tom stirred, then sat up in bed.

"Here's a cup of tea. Are you warm enough now? I think you need to get in the shower again. We've got an hour before breakfast closes; that's if you're hungry."

"Ewan, I'm sorry for putting this on you, but you're the only one I can trust. My uncle in South Africa only gave me the briefest of details. He has a sister company in London who are going to arrange for me to travel by air on Friday to SA. Can you stay in the flat with me till then? They're going to send their chauffeur to pick me up, and I told them you would be with me, and they would have to take you back. Is that okay?"

"Of course."

"And I've been thinking. It would be a great relief if you took over the flat while I'm away. I don't know how long it will be, and I hate to leave it empty and vulnerable. Dad chose it for me. I'll get the locks changed to keep out the bunch you don't like."

"Whatever you want. You're in shock right now, and I guess the malaria shakes didn't help. Stay here for now. I'll go back to the flat and get your pills. Are they still in the bathroom cabinet?"

"If they're not there, try my bedside drawer."

"Once you've settled down, our presentation on Thursday should help take your mind off other things. It's probably best you don't ask for any more details from SA until you get there."

CHAPTER 21

Ewan was first up. The view from the window said it all. Low scurrying clouds trying their best to rain. Tom was asleep but making noises Ewan couldn't decipher. A gentle shake released Tom from another bad dream.

"Kettle's on. We need to leave in an hour. Your bag is in the hallway, but remember you still have to pack your anti-malaria tablets. The shower is all yours. I tried your posh body wash, and it's got quite a pong. Hope it wears off before I meet anyone."

The driver at the door had a hatchet-face look about him, with no attempt at a smile. Perhaps he moonlighted as an undertaker, thought Ewan, though he decided not to share this notion with Tom. They settled in the back seat of an elegant Bentley, which had a glass privacy partition.

"Ewan, I can't get my head round how quickly we can go from extreme happiness to a black hole. Being brought up in Yorkshire was a living dream. From as early as I can remember, we were always having a picnic in the rain, and cycle runs that ended up in a pub, where my dad would make us stand outside whilst he had a pint of their best ale. Mum used to be allowed a gin and tonic as she sat with us outside. We were given ginger beer that we pretended was real ale. My sister used to pour it into the nearest plant pot; she hated the taste. But we all used to laugh. She didn't want to hurt Dad's feelings. Now those memories hurt."

"Well, treat them as treasures that you alone own. You'll need to be strong for your sister, and you can remind her of the good times."

"I know. And thanks for keeping me company. I'll keep you up to speed with what's going on. There was conflict between my dad and his brother in SA, so I'm not sure what to expect from Uncle Jack. I've never really liked him, and Peggy, his wife, is stuffed full of airs and graces, which their finances don't justify. My mother never liked her. The only person I trust is Graham; the guy is company secretary and looks after the company books. Dad always had a high regard for his straight talking and his honesty, and in Cape Town, business and dodginess are the same thing. Dad talked about him taking over the company. I'm not sure what will happen now. My business foundation course won't be that much help."

As the Bentley progressed up the motorway, Ewan was determined to avoid any pregnant pauses that would allow Tom's imagination to return to the fateful phone call. "Tom, I hope I'm not rabbiting on too much, but when I lost my mum and dad, my best friend Fred, though he didn't show emotion, filled all the voids with his encyclopaedic knowledge, and he made sure I listened. He questioned me to make sure my thoughts hadn't wandered, but it took my mind off things; he didn't know how therapeutic it was for me. For starters, let's make sure I know what you think we should include in the presentation. And will you want Eric to take the boat out. We can have a cleaning session without your 'gauleiter' approach."

"Sure. I don't know how long I'll be gone, but please go sailing. I've a copy of the presentation on my laptop, so I can email you my thoughts." Holding hands, out of sight of the chauffeur, meant a great deal to Ewan and gave him a warm glow. At times, he felt the weight of Tom lean into him and was so happy to respond. They had just about covered all the questions Ewan might be asked by the team, including what Ewan should say about the circumstances, when Heathrow came into view.

The chauffeur was getting the luggage from the boot when Ewan held Tom back. "Tom, I've put a letter in your carry-on. Don't open it till you are above the clouds."

"What's in it?"

"Nothing and everything. Remember, I'm here for you, anytime." Their parting was a release of emotion for both of them. The hug lasted a long time.

CHAPTER 22

Tom called Ewan as soon as he arrived in Cape Town. "I'm just about to leave the airport," he said, "and I'm using the driver's phone, so I have to be brief. I can't remember the boarding process; it went by in a haze. I'm still struggling to make sense of where I am and why. My seat was at the front of the plane in First Class and offered a sort of cocoon, but nothing lifted my mood, except that as the aircraft passed through the last layer of clouds, the brightness of the light swamped my space, the seat-belt sign disappeared, and I decided to retrieve your letter from the overhead locker. I must admit my hands were shaking when I opened the envelope. When you said my mind is in a dark place, you were right and that memories would be fighting reality to confuse me. And that's so true. I'm in a bit of a daze. You mentioned your parents, and I expect I'll have similar feelings. I, too, am bloody angry, and, yes, God can take a hike. I don't have a Labrador to confide in, but you'll make a good substitute, and you don't have a cold, wet nose, which helps. Like you say, the pain is unbelievable, and despite my bluff Yorkshire exterior, you're right in pointing out that I'm pretty soft underneath - and you've seen me stark bollock-naked anyway, so I've nothing to hide from you. Thanks for your offer of friendship. It means a lot to me. I may lean on you even more as events develop. I know you're off to Bermuda for the hols to help run your uncle's marina, and the diving school should keep you busy. I just wish I could be there with you; we'd make a good team. Thanks for promising to keep the flat warm for me when I get back, and I agree we are only a Skype or Facetime away. I know we have a lot more to talk about, but it will have to wait. I promise to send you my email address so you can tell me the results of our joint presentation. You didn't embarrass me that it sounded like a love letter, because that's how I took it. People are searching for what I think we have found, and I didn't find it too soppy, as you said. None of it made me uncomfortable, and that's the truth. You can't know what it meant to me. Look, I have to go now. I'll keep you up to date as I find out more. I need a hug."

"Me too. Take care." Ewan put the phone down, warmed by what Tom had said, but convinced there was rough weather ahead. Visions of his own court case crowded in unwanted. He felt sorry he wasn't there to give his support. Ewan knew that Tom could expect the court proceedings to show the robbery scenes in graphic detail, and that he would hear statements that would live in his memory; it would be a personal trial for Tom and never let him relax; he was merely starting the process that Ewan knew only too well.

CHAPTER 23

Ewan's phone rang. It was a foreign number he didn't recognise, and he had a strange, uneasy feeling. "Hello."

"Ewan, I haven't much time. Can you meet me next Sunday at Heathrow? I'm arriving on the BA 129 at nine o'clock. Can you bring an overnight bag to stay with me in London? Oh shit, someone's coming. Don't text me."

"Tom?" The line went dead. Ewan thought Tom's voice was on edge and wondered if he was in trouble. Why shouldn't he text? It was Friday, and Ewan had planned to go sailing with Eric and Claire. They'd understand. Not having heard from Tom for more than a month with their calls hitting an answering machine and all texts unanswered, they were anxious for Tom. It was as if he had disappeared. Even his Facebook page hadn't been updated.

Ewan called Eric and Claire to cancel the sail and described the phone call. They were ready to help whenever and wherever they could, and Ewan promised to keep them up to speed once he had talked to Tom.

Ewan rose as the sun poked through the curtain to start an auspicious Sunday. He made it in time for the six a.m. train to Paddington, then the Heathrow Express, all the while wondering what had happened to Tom. Being early at Heathrow Airport, he roamed the arrival's concourse trying to guess who was meeting whom. Some were pretty obvious from the placards with balloons. Ewan spotted Tom's name on an electronic pad, with the guy holding it wearing a smart chauffeur's hat. Ewan kept his distance by a pillar. He spotted Tom as the doors opened to free the arriving passengers. He was walking hesitantly, with his head swivelling side to side. Ewan waved a hand, and they caught sight of one another. Tom looked weary, as if he had been up all night. His eyes had lost some of their normal sparkle. They hugged.

"God, am I glad to see you, Ewan. Thanks for meeting me. I need you as never before."

"Christ, Tom, you look all in. Let me grab your bags. There's a guy here holding a board with your name on it."

"Okay, I have a lot to talk to you about, but not in front of him. Let's go." They met the chauffeur, and he led the way. The journey to London was in silence. No small talk. Tom took Ewan's hand out of sight of the driver. It sent a tingle through Ewan, and a quick glance at one another filled the passage of time since Tom left.

CHAPTER 24

The car dropped them off at Brown's Hotel in Mayfair. The room was smart and stylish with two huge beds. The décor was expensive understatement. After a welcoming long hug, they sat down.

"Right, Ewan, here's what has happened. When I arrived in SA, I was met by my uncle's secretary, Martha, who I have never liked. Straightaway, I was taken to a cocktail party laid on by my uncle's church group. It was excruciating. They poured sympathy as they poured the drink. When I asked where my sister was, Uncle Jack gave a dismissive wave of his hand, and said she was indisposed at Vineyard House. I was told I was staying with them as our house, Broadview, was still a crime scene. I asked for her telephone number, and that is where my troubles started. At every step after that, they basically closed me down. My old mobile phone was still in the house, and I wasn't allowed access. I asked to buy one, but they insisted I didn't need one. When I arrived at Dad's office, Martha was already there. I asked to see Graham, the company secretary, but she said they had sent him on leave whilst the investigation into the case continued. I managed to get a secretary to give him a message, asking him to get in touch with my sister and arrange a meeting at the vineyard. When I met my sister, she was in a bad way. I've never seen her so withdrawn. We talked about what needed to happen with the funeral and the authorities, but she just told me to help her by taking it all on."

"Was there no one she could turn to?"

"It seemed my uncle's staff were so intrusive that she stopped allowing them into the house. Initially, I wasn't sure why, but my meeting with Graham revealed all. My uncle was trying to get her to sign over her presumed share of the company when the estate is settled. He even had Graham reveal the latest balance sheet; it's a private company so not in the public domain. Graham says that my dad told him to exclude Uncle Jack from all our company dealings, and when Graham attempted to secure the company, he was told where to go. Graham said he didn't know the safe combination, but he did, so removed a copy of my dad's will from the safe and gave it to me. My sister gets the vineyard and the house, and I get the company. They gave me a computer, but somehow, I couldn't email or Skype from my uncle's house. All calls to my old phone just disappeared."

"When I challenged Martha, she said they were just trying to protect me and my sister. Well, Sarah has given me power of attorney for the will-reading at the lawyer's office in Mayfair. And they made all the arrangements for the funeral without asking me. To say they were controlling would be an understatement. I only found details of the incident when Graham showed me the Cape *Mail*. One burglar was shot by the police, and three more were trapped in my dad's Mercedes when it crashed. I'm told the police are under so much pressure and everything in their bureaucratic world goes slow. Even the evidence gathering at the house wasn't finished when I left.

My uncle took over the funeral arrangements after calling the London lawyer to ask what was in the will. Fortunately, the lawyer refused to discuss the will any further until the formal reading here, though he did indicate that cremation was the option. I could have told them that. They arranged everything, so I let them and their church have their way. I wasn't in a position to interfere in a positive way. The ceremony at the crematorium was stark; something my mother would have hated. She loved cut flowers and our house would be overflowing with lupins, gladioli, and roses. She had an intense dislike for lilies, so would have frowned on the ones at the crematorium. Everything was black except the people. Dad wouldn't have approved; he had some terrific black friends who kept him sane, but none had been invited, even the house staff who brought me up. Can you imagine what they must have felt? I seethed inside but couldn't do anything about it. I may go back for the court case. There is the complication that they have to complete the investigation into the robber who was killed, before the main trial can start. I couldn't wait to escape. I've brought the ashes back. Will you go to the Yorkshire moors with me?"

"Of course. We now have the summer break ahead. I don't leave for Bermuda for at least a month."

"The will-reading takes place tomorrow. I've had you appointed as Sarah's representative. I hope you don't mind. Can you come with me?"

"Sure. And when do you want to go to Yorkshire?"

"We can go at the end of the week, once I've settled

back in. I have a company car and driver here. If we go up on Friday, stay overnight at the house, we can be back by Saturday tea-time. Would that be okay? We have a big house in Yorkshire, just outside a village called Goathland in the North Yorkshire Moors, with plenty spare bedrooms if we actually need one. It was when my father worked in oil at Scarborough. I went as weekly boarder to a school near a place called Robin Hood's Bay. Dad thought it would be good for me to be away from home so I would concentrate on my studies, despite home only being an hour away. Mum disagreed but was overruled. I enjoyed being able to have a different life during the week with great mates, then getting back to Mum's brilliant cooking. She spoiled me rotten."

"Well, those are the good memories you need to stack up. It all sounds idyllic."

"It was. Sometimes, I could take the steam-train from nearby Whitby to the North York Moor's railway station near the village. The lads in class were envious. I couldn't have been happier. Then it all changed. We moved to SA because Dad was headhunted to take over an oil supply business that was about to go tits up. My Uncle Jack, who is out there, saw the opportunity but didn't have the money. His lifestyle involved spending money to keep up with those that had it. My dad had the money, so we had to go. I lost all my friends and so did my sister. It was a bloody rude awakening in Cape Town. Apologies, did I go on?"

"No, I'm just sorry I couldn't be with you in SA. You can tell me more detail on the way to Yorkshire, if you want to. I know it's bloody awful waiting for the court case to come round because it triggers off what you've lost. When the court case finally took place for me, I went through all the memories I had tried to hide, but listening to what had happened finally put an end to that chapter; it gives a sort of closure. But all in your own time. Things will be a bit raw for you at the moment."

CHAPTER 25

The lawyer's office in Mayfair looked expensive and, knowing legal charges, probably was. The receptionist was snooty and looked the part. Tom took on the persona of someone who paid her wages, and he had the same approach with the lawyer when they were introduced. Ewan smiled inwardly. The lawyer indicated in a mumble that only related family members were allowed to be at the will-reading.

"This is my close friend, Ewan, and, as you will see from this document, my sister can't be here, but she has appointed him to be her formal representative." It was game, set, and match as the lawyer's eyebrows semaphored surprise and disapproval. "Shall we get on with it? My time is precious, as I'm sure yours is." Tom gave a side glance to Ewan, with a nod to underscore his positivity. Last night, they had decided to be bullish with the elders who seemed to think they had all the answers, and it would give Tom something to aim at.

CHAPTER 26

They set off at seven on a bright Thursday morning for the five-hour journey with overnight bags packed. It was an early start, and the night before had been a passionate reminder of how much they meant to each other. It was as much physical as emotional. Ewan had been desperate to assure Tom that being apart made their bond even stronger, and their bodies had agreed.

At times, Ewan noticed that Tom just stared out of the window, much as Ewan had done during the journey to Invergordon for his parents' funeral. Ewan was in two minds as to whether he should make conversation, but Tom took the initiative about an hour into the journey as they passed a boatyard on the Great Ouse River at Huntingdon on the A1 motorway. "That boatyard reminds me, I took some photos in Cape Town. They're on my phone. Here, have a look; just keep flicking through and say how good they are. The first one is the marina on False Bay which is part of the peninsula that ends in Cape Horn. It's a great location with lots of yachting clubs and boatyards. You can just make out 'Yorkshire Yachts' on the roof of our building. The next picture should be the huge 3D printing machine that makes the hull moulds. It cost a fortune, and came from the US. Dad wanted to be the first. The machine uses carbon fibre reinforced plastic called ABS. We can use some of the photos in our next presentation. I'll shut up and let you flick and be impressed."

"I'm always impressed when I'm with you, but if you see me nod off, it's not because I'm bored; it's because we had another night to remember. You do remember, don't you?"

"Yes. And I didn't drink too much chardonnay. I was still trying to get to know all of you. How come you are so ticklish?"

"Well, no one has touched me like that before. And you have some sensitive spots as well."

"I think there may be more to come, and we still have a long way to go in more senses than one." York Minster was silhouetted against the horizon as they continued northward.

CHAPTER 27

They passed Pickering and followed the A169 towards Whitby. The driver was following the satnav code that Tom had given him. Ewan was captivated by the rolling hills and wooded slopes. The car slowed. The first sign said Cow Wash Beck and the next, Hunt House Road. A larger hoarding had a waterfall picture with the words Mallyan Spout Waterfall. "What's this waterfall about, Tom?"

"That, Ewan, is our destination; it was our paradise in the Dales when Sarah and I were growing up. I'll tell the driver to pull over at this hotel. He'll be staying there."

They both got out. "Follow me. It's about half a mile up this track.'

Ewan let Tom lead him along a defined track with arrows pointing the way ahead. They went through a wood as the sound of rushing water was just making itself heard. Suddenly, they entered a clearing, and facing them was an enormous waterfall.

"What do you think? This is the tallest waterfall in North Yorkshire. We always came here for picnics. Mum and Dad said it was specially made for us, and, at the age of two, we just believed them. It's a run-off from the River Esk. This is where they would want to be." There was a light breeze, and the place had a cathedral-like hush. The trees seemed to deaden any escaping sound. Tom held the small urn closely to his chest. Ewan stood back and tried to fathom the thoughts going through Tom's mind, while attempting to recall how he had been lonely and confused at his parents' funeral. Nobody could help then, but at least he could put a hand on Tom's shoulder to offer support. Tom dropped to his knees on the heather bank, slowly unscrewed the top and let the breeze take the ash over the water. Ewan took a photo for Sarah. Tom stood up and turned to Ewan with a whimsical smile and a shrug of resignation. Then they paused for a selfie, with the waterfall playing gooseberry.

"A good job I took account of the wind. My parents would be laughing if I had got that bit wrong. Thanks for being here. It means a lot to me. We picnicked here as a family, and this was my sister's suggestion; she'll treasure the photo."

"If you want time to yourself, I can wander off a bit."

"No. I need you to be close. This is a long journey, and you've travelled the route before."

"All I can say is that it gets better, though at the time I was just bloody angry."

"I'm done here. Let's get to the house. We'll picnic here sometime, but memories of our fun times are a bit sensitive at the moment. We'll definitely put it in the diary; I want you to feel the joy and warmth I felt here – and I still feel it."

The car entered a single track signed to Hunt House Road, going slowly to avoid the bushes at either side. "Tom, don't you think a Bentley is a bit ostentatious for a Yorkshire lad?"

"Dad said a Rolls-Royce would be over the top, so he went for the Bentley. He wanted to send a message to his chums that he had made it, despite them trying to rubbish him in the local pub."

"Well, I'm getting used to this level of comfort. Just pinch me when I adopt the associated airs and graces."

"Oh. Don't worry, I will."

They turned into a tree-lined avenue, guarded by lions on top of two solid Yorkshire stone pillars. The avenue was impressively lined with dry-stone dykes, with gorse bushes adding a bright yellow carpet. The surrounding land was covered in various different rectangular enclosures with their own dykes; the master plan must have had kinks in it as the rectangles never matched and could form a new guessing board game. "Ewan, this patchwork scenery is my legacy. In any pub discussion on who owns what, you'll hear the locals quote from memory the Tenancy Act of 1670; they love doing that. The Act made sure that the landlords could control all the countryside while pretending to offer grazing land to families who had worked the land. But the victors divided the spoils with the local lordly traitors. It was, and probably still is, an iniquitous legacy: the haves and the have-nots. Don't I sound educated?"

"More on the pompous side, I would say. But now that you mention it, I must be in the 'have-not' clan. In Scotland, everything was owned by the gentry. The Highland Clearances tell it all; I'll give you a lesson on it someday to even the score. But that's all in the past. It's the here and now that we need to focus on. You've now been where I have been. Stone dykes and herds of sheep don't make our destiny, nor should they be allowed to. If we have nothing but only you and me, I feel we've beaten all the odds, and we didn't even gamble; it's a lottery of sorts and we've won. Ewan turned to look at Tom and squeezed his hand. Tom returned a beaming smile.

"What do you think of the scenery?"

"Well, the painter must have dropped his palette. It's pretty grey." The drive opened out onto a large gravel forecourt in front of an impressive grey-stone Georgian mansion, but not a particularly welcome colour to Ewan's eyes. The house extended to either side with enormous wings. Ewan felt it would be difficult to call the place homely. "Golly, Tom. Are we at the right place? This looks eminently too grand for you, and definitely for me."

"This is Esk Hall, Dad's trophy. But a home is where your heart is, and my heart is here with you."

"That's very poetic. But this is a considerable pile in terms of money, status, and size. How many people live here?"

"Look, when we were kids and growing up, my dad entertained like mad. Marquees in the garden, drinks on the lawn, dinners in the hall. He enjoyed entertaining, possibly as a way of getting up the noses of all our relations and the landed gentry. As kids, it was an exciting time; never a dull moment. Mind you, I was co-opted as cheap waiter service. That said, Sarah and I would sneak the dregs from the wine bottles, out of Dad's sight. It was precarious but rewarding labour. When I started to mature a la puberty, he was always inviting his friends who possessed daughters of my age. I was more interested in the boys but didn't dare show that side of me to Dad. I don't think he ever guessed, though I think my mum did."

"And you still don't want to, just like me." Tom nodded.

Standing at the house steps were a grey-haired woman and a bearded man. Tom walked up to them and hugged each. "Ewan, meet my dear friends who looked after me here in my youth. This is Sheila and this is Drew." Ewan was shaken warmly by the hand. Sheila led the way. The entrance hall was imposing and overseen by frowning full-size portraits. Ewan would keep first impressions to himself.

"Thanks, Sheila. I'll take Ewan upstairs and show him what you always called the nursery. As you can see, I've grown a little since then. We'll be down on the dot of twelve." Sheila just stood there looking at Tom with watering eyes.

"Let's go upstairs." Tom led the way up a baronial staircase to a gallery with rooms around the periphery. Pausing outside one door, he bowed slightly. "Welcome to my bedroom. All my dreams started here, so you'll have to excuse me if I get a bit sentimental."

The room was massive with a four-poster bed plonked in the middle. All the wood surrounds consisted of twisted walnut carvings and friezes, in contrast to the acres of teenage posters and sailing memorabilia covering every wall. The windows had a veranda opening out to a lakeside view, absolutely stunning. Ewan's eyes were already on stilts. "Don't be fooled. The view might be to die for, but if you are lonely, it means bugger all. Sometimes, I craved for what the lads at boarding school had with their home-spun fun and brothers and sisters. Okay, I had Sarah, but we didn't see eye to eye all the time. She enjoyed the country set; I didn't. And she had a wardrobe, call it a closet, and I used to hide in it and jump out and scare her. Now, I want to stay in the closet, so don't laugh."

"Would I?"

"You are seeing my secrets that nobody else has ever seen, except my mum; Dad wasn't allowed in here. I think I've outgrown most of it except my record collection. It's mainly classical, so may not be to your taste."

"What do you mean? I used to prance around to Ride of the Valkyries, and I would play Holst and his Planets at full volume. I think it was one of the few sounds that Fred enjoyed. So, you see, I'm slightly educated on the popular scale. I expect you're more into Mozart and Mendelssohn."

"No, I like Borodin and I love the picture he paints of the Russian steppes – it's escapism for me. We must go there some day, but right now lunch calls. You might be able to guess what we're having. Sheila makes the most – oops, I almost gave the game away. Wait and see. Between them, Sheila and Drew are the most helpful couple you could imagine. As kids, we were spoiled by them – in secret; Dad never knew about the toffees and syrup sponge we sneaked to the summer house. Once we've eaten, I'll have a quick chat with them and explain that nothing changes. It will be my great bolthole, or can I say ours. Then I'd like to walk the paths I did as a kid. I know it sounds terribly sentimental, but I need to grab hold of something, as well as you. Looking back, I realise I was lonely then. If you can stomach a trip down memory lane, I promise to keep a stiff upper lip. I don't think we'll be able to get here often, so I want to make sure you see what I see, when I start to reminisce. Time's almost up. I know Shelia has been busy in the kitchen, and she will have made a superb lunch, but don't eat too much; later, we'll have to do her dinner justice, and you'll be surprised at lunch for starters." And Ewan was. They both grinned when she brought in the enormous plate of Yorkshire pudding and a full gravy boat. Tom pointed to the pile and grinned. "This is proper food. It'll set you up for any journey, and we need to make a dent in it so as not to cause offence. Help yourself." They didn't realise how hungry they were, and justice was done. "Come on, I need to show you more of my childhood."

Ewan was impressed as they walked through the downstairs rooms. A huge sitting room led into a ballroom that fronted the house, while a long library lined the back. Huge French windows opened out onto magnificent views over a well-manicured lawn. The view continued with lakes, and the dales beyond were deep green, the stuff of country magazines. There was a smell of polish and leather everywhere.

"Tom, it can't be cheap having a housekeeper and ghillie on permanent call. How can you manage it, if it's not too rude to ask?"

"Well, Sheila and Drew are a couple and have been at Esk Hall for as long as I can remember. Dad kept them on after we left to make sure the place stayed in good order so that he could drop in at any time. Eventually, the place was turned into a summer venue for company gatherings that needed peace and quiet, and there are tons of that here. The arrangement breaks even, and Sarah and I always have a welcoming bolthole."

Tom led Ewan past the boatshed by the side of the lake to a small copse on the lee of a hill. As they breached the hill, there, in front of them, was a go-cart track. Tom grinned. "Dad was a little eccentric as my mother would attest to. He got hooked on carts, as you will see when we get back to the garage. You won't believe that Sarah holds the record here."

Ewan felt that Tom was relishing the chance to show off his past in a natural way, without any hint of boasting. The peace being generated would only last until they returned to uni, but it was worth savouring the moment. They came to the large garage, and Tom gingerly opened the doors. Drew had suggested getting the carts out, and Tom just beamed at the idea. They entered the garage to the smell of high-octane fuel. Drew had readied two carts, one with pink paintwork. "This place is special, 'cos it represents the fun we used to have. Dad was forever tinkering here. Look, here are the carts, and before you say anything, the pink one is Sarah's, the Pink Terror. Dad made sure it was always better tuned than the others. When my mates came for the weekend, they always shied away from the Pink Terror, and so I won lots of races. Mind you, Sarah used to enjoy showing them her back wheels. Being lighter than them, they didn't stand a chance. It was great to see their expressions when they were beaten by a girl. Let's draw lots as to who goes in pink. Which hand do I have the key in?"

"Your left one."

"Yes, so you're in pink."

"Hang on, what's in your right hand?"

"The key to the other one." Tom laughed, knowing they were both the same.

Ewan had difficulty keeping up as Tom's cart led the way around the back of the house. He hadn't tried a cart before, and it was a rapid and steep learning curve, just like the track. An hour of practice ended with a race. It was almost their first squash match over again. The Pink Terror seemed eager to respond, and Tom's jibes just egged Ewan on. Tom had the edge until the last lap, when he went slightly wide as he shouted at Ewan to keep up. The goad was enough for Ewan to cut the corner in a slide and become the pink champ. The laughter was an antidote to the solemnity of the morning ritual. Drew welcomed them back, as he had done Tom very many years ago.

Tom was true to his word about dinner. The table sported a huge salmon, surrounded by massive bowls of vegetables, all fresh, Sheila had stated, from the garden. Ewan eyed the bowl of new potatoes sporting a covering of rosemary. Ewan had never had such a feast laid before him. "Ewan, are you happy to have some SA chardonnay to complement Sheila's finest Yorkshire cooking."

"You bet. Thank you, Sheila. This looks delicious. We won't be able to make it up the stairs." Sheila just beamed and patted Tom on the shoulder. It was a touching moment. She had a tear in her eye.

They made it upstairs, with Tom carrying another bottle of chardonnay and two glasses. "Ewan, I'm beginning to relax. Thanks for all the help. Sheila wanted to make sure you sampled her Yorkshire cooking. At times, she was a surrogate mother to Sarah and me. It was a horrendous parting when we left. I hope she's always here for me, for us. Let's ruffle the bed clothes in your room for appearances' sake, then we can relax in mine. I'd love to watch one of my old films with you. How about *Dr. Zhivago*? It's escape music, and we can get used to 'Borodin' scenery."

"I couldn't be happier. And a four-poster will be a first for me, though I don't know if I will last to the end."

CHAPTER 28

They stirred as the sun poked its rays into the bedroom, and Ewan murmured," How was last night for you?"

"Hopefully, the same as for you. Heaven doesn't get much better, though you didn't make it all the way through *Lara's Theme*. I may have been a distraction."

"You were, but I'll always associate that film with my best night in Yorkshire. I only hope we didn't make too much noise."

"It's okay. Sheila and Drew's rooms are miles away, and the music would have drowned anything out. It was great to relax again. Days like yesterday are duty, and I think it was duty well done. Right, you take first tilt at the bathroom. I'll check the news, then we can see what Sheila has in store for us. She said she'll do us a goody bag for the journey. The driver is due to pick us up at ten."

The breakfast was as impressive as last night's dinner. The aromas of cooking bacon and fried bread engulfed both of them as they faced a gargantuan spread. Tom popped out to speak to Drew as Sheila was pointing out what each dish was, and then whispered, "Tom has probably mentioned our association with the past, and we hope the future. When I first saw him yesterday, he seemed to have a big weight on his shoulders; remember, I've known him since he pooped his pants, and I now see a beautiful young man. With the tragedy, he may be fragile inside; I've seen him put on a bluff Yorkshire exterior before, when they had to up sticks. You appear to have a good influence on him; he trusts you. Please look after him. He means a lot to us."

"I certainly will. I've been where he is, and I know how it feels. We have a little team at uni; we look after one another."

"I know, and I shouldn't say, and Drew would kill me for interfering, but I sense something different between you two. It makes me feel good and happy for his future."

"Tom is special to me. We've both been through a loss that few people experience. I guarantee to do my best for him."

"Thanks. Here he comes."

Tom's farewells of Sheila were touching and sad. They had seen happier times together, and Ewan could tell the visit had meant a great deal to them both. He, too, felt the poignancy of the moment. As they drove away, Tom didn't say anything, and Ewan felt a pang of sympathy. He remembered the feeling from a time long ago.

The day had been overflowing with emotions, which had taken their toll on them both. Sleep invaded their thoughts as they leaned against one another on the way back.

The slowing down of the car as they entered Southampton broke into their different worlds. "Well, that was a momentous day. Thanks for being with me. I couldn't have done it on my own. I hope it wasn't too hard on you. At least you got to sample proper Yorkshire pudding, and we have a stash of food to last the week."

"You can say that again. I'll book an early evening slot for the squash court. We need to work off all that food, and I need to loosen up a bit. You can unwind after such a hectic and pressurised couple of days. And tomorrow is our lecture hall practice run with the team, which should be fun. I'm not saying Thursday's presentation will be easy, but if we rehearse enough, we might get through."

"Remember, I'm booked on Monday's flight to SA, so once Thursday is out of the way, we have a few evenings on our own, except for the sailing trip which doesn't count, and that means more than I can say. I hope you feel the same."

"Can't you guess? But before then and on a mundane level, we still have to review the slides. Eric and Claire are coming over after lunch, so let's get the gear set up."

"Right, the projector is in the cupboard next to my suitcase. I'm just about packed."

"How long will you be away for?"

"Not sure, but I am going back to kick ass, to use your words. I'm bloody angry at the way they treated me, so my uncle will quickly understand that I'm now streetwise, and my first actions will be to get Graham back to running the company, with the locks changed, followed by a full tour of inspection of Yorkshire Yachts. The London lawyer has already emailed a copy of the will. That should get that cow of a woman to mind her manners. Anyway, I'll talk it through with you so that I have a detailed plan as I hit the ground there. You can always put another letter in my carry-on. I can't say what that meant to me."

CHAPTER 29

The four of them spent most of the afternoon fine-tuning the slides. Tom was to top and tail, Ewan to describe the project, Eric to give the underlying engineering theory, and Claire to outline the marketing strategy, with Tom finishing off with the financials. The uni became the focus of their joint minds. The lecture room on the top floor, Level 3, had great views over the River Itchen. It would be a good perch for blue-sky thinking, but its setting was akin to a Star Chamber. Their presentation to the judges was scheduled for ten o'clock on Thursday.

"Right, Tom. Kick it off." Claire sounded quite officious.

"Okay, but I need the bloody slide to point at."

"Let's relax, guys," Ewan said softly. "All we need to do here is get our confidence. We've made the content over the months; now we have to deliver a slick presentation."

After many stops and starts, they began to develop a buzz from each other. Tom occasionally stuttered in his enthusiasm, and Eric developed a professorial voice that made them laugh. Claire had a hard job stopping it from being a boys-only show, reminding them they might have developed an engineering marvel, courtesy of Fred, but that the presentation was to sell their idea convincingly to the judges, and she wasn't yet convinced. They made faces.

By dinnertime, they were almost there, with Tom uncorking a bottle of wine to help them relax. Eric was already working on amendments to the slides, and Claire re-drafted the script to make it flow better. They had three days to get it right.

Ewan was in the kitchen doing a session of washing-up when Claire edged into his peripheral vision. "Now, Claire, you've not come to relieve me, have you?"

"Not exactly, you're doing a grand job on your own. But I just thought I would mention that you and Tom always seem to be at loggerheads on the boat and during our debriefs. Is it that you beat him at squash more times than he wins, or is it something deeper? It would be great to sew more harmony; we have still a long way to go."

"Right, Claire. In vino veritas, and I swear you to secrecy on pain of death and my option to tell everyone of your crush on Eric."

"Crush on Eric? Nonsense," she said, her face bright red.

"Tom and I like one another but don't want to show or make it public, so we lean the other way. He's been through hell, and I have a little experience of that place, so I give him quiet support. We would rather not be seen doing anything to give any other impression. I know that's a bit convoluted to say something I could probably say in a more direct way. Does that make sense?"

"I'm relieved 'cos I like you both equally. Eric doesn't know about me, I don't think, so all three of us can stay shtum. Agreed?"

"All four of us if you count Eric." Claire chuckled. "Do you agree? And I think you and Eric would make a great pair, but then I'm not an expert in that field, yet. Let's make the most of what we have here. It's all I need at the moment, and you're an important part of it." Ewan was rewarded with a kiss on the cheek, and he duly blushed.

All was set for the challenge on Thursday as they left the flat, with little jobs to complete before then. It would help being second on the list, giving the judges time to settle in. Tom promised breakfast in the flat to make a good start.

CHAPTER 30

The uni common room was buzzing, with the presentation teams milling about. Anxious faces stared at paperwork. The odd tantrum escaped from a group, and a few teams seemed to be arguing among themselves. The results of the presentations were critical for the credits they gave each individual as part of the degree process. But acting as a business team carried kudos with the judges.

"I think our weakest point is the 'financials'. When Tom presents them at the end, we might be asked for greater detail, so you'll have to use Fred's analysis. You can tell them that the idea of a small flying boat isn't new, but electric power and carbon fibre, with its green credentials, are a step change for saving costs. I'm calling the project FRED, Flying Boat Re-engineered for Electric Drive Trains. I realise that sounds pretty contrived, which it is, but we owe it to recognise Fred's constant input. I don't know if he'll appreciate the significance, but it'll make me feel good."

With nods all round, Eric set off to do the necessary, being the slide-master. They waited in the hallway, clear of the opposition. Eric arrived back, puffing. "You lot with your last-minute changes will do my heart in."

"Now, now, Eric," cooed Claire, "just think you did it for me." Eric's face went red.

"Here's the updated first slide. I've put FRED in capitals emerging from a choppy sea, with a suitable decode at the bottom. Everyone happy?"

"Yes, and remember, we need to keep the emphasis on 'green'. We won't mention Fred as our absent guru." At the back of his mind, Ewan would always be protective of Fred; their relationship was deep down inside and not for public inspection.

As they filed into the small lecture room, it reminded Ewan of walking into court. It looked unfriendly, and the three judges looked hard-faced and serious. It had definitely been a good idea to drop Eric's jokes, and there ought to be no ad-libbing. Tom placed the slides on the viewer platform, took a deep breath, and switched the power on. There was a brief flash of light then darkness. Tom started to stutter. "For f- f..." Thankfully, the swearword didn't make it out. Eric found and changed the fuse. "My apologies. Our subject is about an electric aircraft, and as you will guess, we are at an early stage, but have built redundancy in, and we have more spare fuses in our back-pocket." The judges seemed to relax as Tom started the proceedings.

Forty-five minutes later, after batting some penetrating questions, Tom was winding up the presentation, when the middle judge, a frosty-looking, peroxide blonde of indeterminate age, challenged the financial aspects. Fred had done a brilliant job on a costing analysis, and the spreadsheet was as complicated as it was detailed. They had decided a summary was enough; obviously not for her. Tom called for the detailed slide and proceeded to take her through the assumptions, the full expenditure, and the contingency planning. Halfway through the slide she gave in with a studied nod. They were finished, and trooped out not knowing how they had fared.

"Back to the flat for a celebratory drink; I've some bottles on ice. And I think we did well. How about you lot?"

Eric and Claire were beginning to smile. Ewan had been cornered by the form tutor, but as he strode back, he gave a thumbs-up. "Our tutor seems to think Miss Peroxide, from the Institute of Accountants, was bowled over by the huge spreadsheet. The explanatory notes, by the gift of Fred, touched the right spots. We have a week to wait for the results. Let's celebrate."

CHAPTER 31

After the celebratory drinks session, the others eventually left with a promise to depart the sailing club dock at eight o'clock the following morning for a final sail with Tom round the Lymington Spit buoy; they were intent on setting a record, and the predicted winds looked favourable. Ewan and Tom had time to themselves. The elephant in the room was Tom's impending departure for SA.

"Right, Tom, I need a plan or at least a timetable. You are off on Monday to SA, and I'm off the following Friday to Bermuda to make some money."

"Look, I have stacks of dosh, so you don't have to pimp yourself playing dockhand to your uncle. Come with me to Cape Town. I've hired security, so we would be safe as houses. Okay, not houses, that was a bad call, but the guys we have engaged have a good pedigree and come well recommended. Graham has used them before when my dad received intel that a new bunch were establishing themselves in the Cape, and there were Mafia connections. The oil business was said to be one of their targets. I now feel much safer than my last visit."

"It's not that I don't want to be with you 'cos I do more than ever; it's just that I've already committed to Uncle Bert, and Archie relies on me to get the diving programme under way. I feel obliged. We can stay in touch, and absence makes the heart grow fonder, doesn't it?"

"Suppose so, but I still have to work out how to handle Dad's affairs. Sarah still wants me to do whatever I think best. She's safe with her boyfriend and doesn't want to be reminded of the past; she has recurring nightmares."

"So do you. I can't tell who you're shouting at in your sleep, but I wouldn't want to be on the receiving end. I thought our relaxed sailing with the team would get rid of your demons, but I guess it'll take time. If you kick arse when you get there, it might be therapeutic."

"The clan in SA don't know when I'm coming, and I've sworn Graham to secrecy. He has arranged a private meeting with the accountants, and I've told the stuck-up London lawyer to do nothing until I decide what to do. There's an SA lawyer who was a close golfing partner of my dad, so we'll use him to take over the SA end. I've never been so fired-up about anything else before."

"Oh, so I come second, do I?"

"Look, Ewan, it's you that's made me fired-up. You can't come second to yourself. I need you like never before, and I enjoy planning for that. Once SA is sorted, and you've done your duty, we can get back to uni and make that boat-plane fly or sail. Agreed?"

"Agreed. To bed. We've an early start on the water in the morning, and won't return here till Sunday evening. Have you finished re-packing for Monday? I saw you have piles of different shorts and shirts on the bed."

"I'm almost there. I've decided to tone my colours down; don't want to appear too brash."

"With those designer labels, I don't think you could. Now, I know you don't want me to come to the airport, so Monday morning needs to be stress free. As you don't get picked up until late afternoon, I thought an early morning bike-ride to the flying boat museum would remind you why you want to come back here after sorting out SA. Deal?"

"Deal, but tonight I need ..."

CHAPTER 32

The farewells were torture for them both, and the hugs lasted just short of forever. As the car pulled away, Ewan's eyes were watering, and his chest was heaving. The emotion of the parting took its toll on him. He felt wrung out and deflated. They had just spent an idyllic time together and the break was mean. The return to an echoing flat said it all. Ewan busied himself tidying up before the cleaning lady arrived; he didn't want her to get the impression standards might drop. He paused as he was straightening the duvet cover. The night before had been a jumble of arms and legs; their bodies had found one another, and few words were needed; it was more than just warmth. They kissed as never before, and whispered thoughts passed between them. Ewan had never felt such a bond, though a flashback to Fred's unwavering loyalty hit his memory banks. He had loved Fred in a different way, but it was love all the same. They had fallen asleep to their own magic.

Now, with Tom gone, and as he arranged the books on the desk, a photo album at the bottom of the pile managed to end up on the floor. It was open at a page displaying two photos – one showing what Ewan took to be Tom's parents, his sister, and Tom standing next to someone, but the photo had been cropped to remove whoever it was. The other photo showed Tom's sister with a man, as well as Tom standing next to someone who had also been cropped, but there was part of a dress left. Something personal must have been going on to take such drastic action. Tom had never mentioned any of his friends in SA, so Ewan was intrigued but decided to close the album, and store the question for a later date.

CHAPTER 33

Ewan was finishing his shower when he heard the phone ring. He knew it could only be Tom at that time in the morning. Still dripping, he managed to get his slippery hands to it. Tom's voice sounded a long way away, and it was.

"Hello, South Africa, from a wet body that you know."

"Sorry, did I catch you at an awkward moment, as I usually do?"

"Yes, but the floor's now wet so it doesn't matter. It's bloody good to hear your voice. I'm all ears."

"Ewan, thanks for putting that picture of us both in my carry-on. It meant a lot to me. From the background, I'm guessing it was at the waterfall in Yorkshire. Don't worry, I'm not lost now, but I've decided to cut from SA. A lot has gone on here, and most of it isn't good. I don't think I'm safe. My sister has completely changed, even with improved security at Vineyard House, and she still thinks we're vulnerable to the robbers' families. The family of the one that the police killed has been making threats to the company. I've let Graham take over the consultancy for a nominal sum. He has the right contacts and is strong enough to keep Uncle Jack at bay. My dad's yacht-building business is in excellent shape, with a full order book, but I want to keep it at arm's length; they know what they're doing, and I trust them. There is quite a bit of money, so, once I've finished at uni, we can set something up. What do you think?"

"By the way, I'm well, so thanks for not asking."

"Sorry. Apologies. It's just been hectic here, and I wanted to offload on you as soon as possible. So, how are you?"

"Well, the flat's in good shape but feels empty. I'm making sure the cleaning lady can't find any dust. Eric and Claire have been over, and we've talked a lot about you. Your ears must have been burning. We've done some sailing; Eric has his ticket, and Claire has one exam to do. I'm further behind, but the uni project of the flying boat is taking shape. I sent you the report on our presentation. Our tutor says it was one of the best, and we have gained all the predicted credits, so all worth the effort. Since then, Fred's input has been extraordinary, and he is now a fluid dynamics expert. When you get back, I'm dying to show you his contribution. And mentioning coming back …"

"Right. I've decided to sail my dad's yacht back to the UK, and I know that will sound odd and wasn't in the plan. I've been out quite a few times as you could tell by my pics. It's perfect for ocean going, and it has every gizmo and self-aid under the sun. It has built-in security, and part of the cabin can be converted quickly to a citadel. The whole design revolves around the well-heeled who feel vulnerable and some very neat aero/nautical dynamics; you'll be impressed. The security aspect is one of its best-selling points, so I'll be safe. My dad used to let me do my own thing, and all he did was monitor safety issues. His debrief was always encouraging, and I won a few races with it. I aim to leave after my sister's wedding in a month's time. Jerry is perfectly suited for her, and they are madly in love. I didn't know they've been going out in secret for three years. Mum and Dad never mentioned it. At least she has great support since the robbery. And she is pregnant, which I hear has got the church clique talking."

"That's caught me by surprise, but it's good news about Sarah. A sailing trip should take the pressure off you, though I'm not too sure about you sailing solo all the way back to the UK. It's a bloody long way, and I won't be able to help. Can't you get it shipped and fly back?"

"Strange you should say that. No. I think my dad would have wanted me to do it. It will be for him and should be cathartic – a word you've used before. It'll exorcise some of my demons. The yacht was shipped to Rio for its annual service, and Dad had arranged to upgrade the engines. So, the starting point is Rio. I'll fly there soon, and do some local sailing with the club there to get my hand in. Then I'll aim for the Azores, and when I bump into them, I'll let you know. The final leg will be to the UK. I'm not sure of the timing, but the closer I get, we can be more accurate, provided the Bay of Biscay doesn't play silly buggers."

"Okay, I'll be with you all the way, in spirit at least. Let's talk before you depart. Is there anything I can do at this end? Remember, I'll be in Bermuda in a week's time earning my spending money for the next year. I should be able to track your GPS signal; just don't get lost. I need you for the first semester; you're crucial to the project, and I need your vote, and your body."

"I have to go. My sister is waving at me to lock up the house. We're having dinner with her boyfriend's parents. I haven't met them, so this is a first. Wish me luck. I'll keep you posted."

The line went dead. Ewan was trying to get his head around what Tom was attempting. Tales of the treacherous South Atlantic passage were littered with failed dreams. Bermuda was a big recipient of limping yachts, broken masts, and torn sails. Something was obviously goading Tom, but the solitude gave Ewan cause for concern. What if his defences were down and the malaria symptoms returned? Encouragement would have to be unconditional. Ewan emailed Tom his full support and asked for the route plan, so he could do some research. It would be a trying time for both of them, and he was missing Tom more than he would let on, but didn't want to add to his burden by saying so. It would have to wait for a better time and place, and Bermuda was calling.

Tom emailed his route, which, at least, didn't involve the notorious Cape Horn, and making Rio the launch point took the sting out of some of the journey. Ewan researched the possible routes and noticed some skirted the Bermuda Triangle, but Tom's route to the Azores would keep him well clear.

CHAPTER 34

Suitably installed in some very basic accommodation, a converted forty-foot container with all mod cons at Paradise Harbour, Ewan's Bermuda adventure was just beginning. Archie, Uncle Bert's sidekick, met Ewan and gave him a warm welcome. "It's great to see you again. You can carry on where we left off last year. I've stocked your fridge and my missus has prepared for your appetite. I'll go through any changes from last year. Let's get to the pub and work out a timetable."

"Well, it's good to see you again, Archie. I think you're hiding behind a bigger beard. I can't tell whether you're smiling or not. That could prove difficult if I make a mistake. I'm not as wet behind the ears as I'm now at uni in Southampton. I won't bore you with the details, suffice to say my subject is fluid dynamics so I may nag you for info. I need all the help I can get."

"That sounds very grand. I just hope your hands haven't gone soft."

"No chance. I've taken to sailing in a big way, and a group of us sail most weekends. I'll need your advice to get ahead of them. Actually, one of them already has a deep-sea qualification and is sailing his father's yacht back soon from

Rio to the UK. It would be great if you could help me track his position. He said he has the latest gizmos so he shouldn't get lost."

"As long as he backs everything up with common sense, he might make it. The Atlantic can be quite unforgiving."

Ewan felt his tummy do a flip. "Bloody hell, I hope the gods are kind to him. The yacht's state of the art."

"We often get 'state of the art' in here with something dangling off."

Ewan looked hard at Archie. "Well, we can log on to his transponder and keep a check on his progress, can't we?"

"Sure, the office has all the up-to-date equipment. We can probably download a version to your laptop. Let's go to the pub, and I'll bring some charts, then we can meet in the office after your first class tomorrow to start the process."

Ewan logged on to the tracking software and entered Tom's call-sign. The associated transponder relay lit up, and he saw what appeared to be some proving runs out of Rio and back. With daily checks nothing seemed to be happening until, on the third day, one of the tracks continued north-eastwards for some distance, and Ewan guessed the trip was underway. Ewan had spoken to Archie about the yacht, the background, and what was at stake. Archie suggested they should plot the progress on the charts at the club, with Archie overlaying the weather forecast each day to get a feel for the sea conditions. The club members always needed a project to criticise. At least Ewan would be able to sympathise with Tom as he battled the elements, albeit from a posh clubhouse. Ewan's internet signal sometimes disappeared for hours, which sent Ewan hot footing it to the dock office for an update. They were a friendly bunch, and he was basically a native by association. Their huge antenna was a league more sophisticated than Ewan's lock-on to a neighbour's internet connection. If Ewan became agitated, Archie would always calm him down with his nautical know-how and calming slow Scottish voice. Nothing seemed to faze him, and as the permanent life-boat skipper, he was ideal for the role.

Bermuda was an oasis of islands, and St George's Harbour stretched for miles. The Royal Navy used the place as a sanctuary from the Atlantic storms and hurricanes. Uncle Bert had joined the Scottish contingent that occupied Paradise Cove on the west side of Paget Island. Becoming the local harbour master was his life's ambition, and he made it when he married the local minister's daughter. It was a marriage cemented by generous donations to the church roof. The diving centre in a cove within walking distance of the harbour became a posh venue that saw the great and the good come from St Georges to enjoy the sheltered surroundings and the terrific banks of fish that took refuge in the complicated series of rockfalls. Ewan liked the setting, and the challenge it gave him. Lighthouse Hill always reminded him of the Lochain Hills, a lifetime away.

The whole area was steeped in history. Every explorer and his dog had bumped into the island and left some legacy. The only shadow on the horizon was the notorious Bermuda Triangle. Ewan decided it was better not to ask.

He was kept busy. His new PADI qualification allowed him to earn more money on the tuition side at the diving school. Uncle Bert was a hard Scot but appreciated being able to lie in on a morning whilst Ewan opened the marina and unlocked the fuel pumps. Ewan's accommodation, the converted container, came from a shipwreck, courtesy of the previous year's hurricane. All the kids had yellow bikes from one of the containers. Ewan's container was surprisingly user-friendly. Holes had been cut out to make windows with the metal re-used to provide hurricane-proof battens. It had all mod cons with running water, and full electric power made the air conditioning unit efficient, yet noisy.

He enjoyed his quirky accommodation, and being at the edge of the marina, he was not only on the job but also close to the inshore rescue centre. He was a volunteer on the rescue rigid inflatable, and the weekly practice provided great camaraderie. The emergency frequency was piped to the loudspeakers around the marina and harbour, and the unannounced callouts were part of the excitement.

Ewan lost track of Tom's journey after two weeks. The GPS signal had disappeared. Without any idea what had happened, Ewan was on edge. He called Graham in SA to see if he had heard anything but couldn't get through. The signs were ominous. Archie, on the other hand, was upbeat remarking that sailing never went to plan and electronics were the bane of the modern sailing fraternity. There was nothing Ewan could do. Impotent and worried, he concentrated on work. Ewan had discussed Tom's intended journey and continually sought Archie's advice. Archie seemed to know by intuition that there was more to Ewan's interest in Tom's progress than appeared to an outsider. Archie went out of his way to keep Ewan occupied from dawn till dusk to fill the void, and the two debated the route as if they had planned it themselves

There was continual talk about the vagaries of the weather, and the Bahamas were on hurricane alert. Bermuda might get some backlash, so securing every piece of equipment became a priority. Ewan's mobile home was well anchored to the concrete base with old steel hawsers that formed robust anchors; it was a perfect home in a storm. The window covers providing full protection were the original steel, and the forty-foot container was going nowhere. Ewan felt safe, knew that Tom wasn't, and all he could do was worry. He just hoped Tom was ahead of the hurricane's path as the winds in the Bahamas were increasing dramatically. At least here in Bermuda, they should avoid the worst. Tom had two emergency locator beacons, so if there was an emergency, they would know. This still left Ewan uneasy.

Ewan was walking back from unlocking the marina gates when the loudspeakers crackled into life. The short-wave emergency frequency repeated a call from a yacht close to Devil's Point with a broken rudder. The rocks in the area were a notorious trap in what looked like an inviting bay. There was quite a swell working the waves in the harbour. The klaxon sounded, and Ewan ran to the muster station and grabbed his wetsuit. Others arrived quickly, and they were on their way in minutes. Archie was duty coxswain with four others on board. Ewan was the junior but had earned their respect. The shouted brief was "Devil's Rock bay to capture a drifting fifty-footer". Ewan's main job was heaving a line. He had plenty of practice from the harbour wall, and won the local competition at lassoing a motorised inflatable. He was ready in the bow.

They turned Devil Point Head and in the swell Ewan could just make out the yacht's profile. It was very close to Ragged Rock, and Archie gunned the RIB to get between the Rock and the yacht. They closed and Ewan could see a figure in the prow. Ewan threw with all his strength to get the bobbin over the yacht's metal guard-rail. The figure caught it and reeled in the main sheet to fix it to the deck capstan; the tow began. It was a big swell, and they made slow but safe progress into the calm of the harbour. As Ewan shortened the lead to get the yacht closer, he shouted to the figure to keep the line taut. The voice that replied was very familiar.

"What the fuck are you doing here?" Ewan shouted.

"It's a long story, but I was looking for you."

"Shit. I told you to fly. We could have had a happy ending in the UK."

"I feel like crap. Can you get me out of this peapod? I've been rolling around since the rudder parted."

"Step over and take my hand. It's all moving, but I promise to catch you – again." He felt a thrill to be holding Tom's hand. Tom was just thanking the crew, and offered to help with securing the yacht, when Archie, sensing something, told Ewan to get Tom to the medical centre pronto as his shaking was giving him cause for concern. The Doc, Old Ted, rapidly diagnosed the after-effects of malaria and dictated bed-rest. Ewan took pleasure in inviting Tom to his "house". They were both too knackered to discuss the merits of a container home. All Tom kept saying was, "I wanted to surprise you," and Ewan kept saying, "You did."

Tom was shaking and shivering as Ewan prodded him to the bed. "Have you taken your pills?"

"No, I've left them in the cabin; they're in the chart-desk drawer."

"Okay, I'll go and get them. Lie down, and sleep. You're safe here in my rustic, hurricane-proof shed. Breakfast is served at seven a.m." Their hug and kiss didn't need words. "We'll talk in the morning over fresh coffee." But Tom was already asleep.

The yacht was safe and secure in the inner harbour. Ewan noticed that the name on the yacht was *Scarborough Fair*, very appropriate for a Yorkshire owner. It truly was magnificent and top-of-the-range. The superstructure was covered in aerials and radars. Even in the dull weather, the hull gleamed, and the steel shone. As Ewan entered the cabin, he could sense how lonely it must have been for Tom. The navigation desk was immaculate, as was all the furniture inside, but too sterile. Pulling open the desk drawer, Ewan located the pills, and there were tons of them. He wasn't sure how bad Tom's malaria side effects were, but the pills said it all. Just as he closed the drawer, Ewan noticed a pin-board with the daily log printed out together with weather forecasts, and Post-it notes, and to the top corner, half hidden, was a photo of Ewan smiling. It was one of the selfies they took in the flat on their first meeting. Ewan felt a tug at his heart, and a warmth of recognition.

CHAPTER 35

Tom woke at lunchtime, drowsy and disorientated. "It's me - your buddy Ewan. You're in my bed in a shipping container in Bermuda."

"Where? Shit, I have a stonking headache."

"You're in Bermuda with your best mate."

"So, it was you shouting at me. Have I been a pain in the neck?"

"Only because I wasn't expecting you. You were supposed to be sailing to the Azores across the Atlantic for the UK. What changed?"

"I just wanted to surprise you."

"Well, you definitely did. You only just made it before Devil's Rock ate you. Archie has already had a look at your rudder. The kingpost is fractured and has pulled the stainless-steel rings through the carbon fibre. It's a simple repair job once we get the composite work done. It will take a little time, and the weather forecast for the next two weeks includes the arse-end of a hurricane. So, you'll be stuck here with me."

"That was my plan. The pills will get me up and about in no time."

"First, are you going to have a shave? You have hair on

your face that I've seen somewhere else."

"You shouldn't have been looking. It's private."

"That's not what you said before. And remember, I did give you a compliment or has your memory gone with the rudder pins?"

"Okay, I'll have a shave if it makes you happy. I thought the Ancient Mariner look suited me."

"If you recall, the Ancient Mariner story didn't have a happy ending. I want a happy ending. Right. Get better quickly and help me with the precocious kids in the diving school class. Their parents pay good money, but they are little, moneyed, pushy brats. They take after their parents. It will get you back on an even keel. You must have spent the last few weeks at an angle."

"You bet. Can I help with the repair, or anything else?"

"No, just recover to normal. We'll visit Archie in the workshop, and you can talk through the repair. He's a wizard welder, is the major domo of the marina, and a lifeboat coxswain. He is from Scotland and may not take to a Yorkshireman, so mind your Ps and Qs. When you're ready we can visit the yacht, empty the bogs, and do a spring-clean. By the way, I like the name."

"Oh, that was Dad's idea. His first major job in oil saw him operate out of there, and as kids we would always sing 'Are we going to Scarborough Fair?', and Dad would always say, 'Someday'."

"It suits. We will get there 'Someday', I promise. We can attack the chores tomorrow so we can have an early night. We have lots to catch up on and make up for, if you know what I mean."

"That's why I'm smiling."

CHAPTER 36

"That was some night after a busy day. You look better this morning. What did you think of Archie? I thought he has already worked wonders with the rudder links, and the welded kingpost should be here by the end of the week. I've registered your arrival with the harbour master, as it happens, my Uncle Bert. He said we are invited to the sailing club's barbeque tomorrow. They're a bit snooty until you get to know them, and there's lots of money about, so you should be in your element. We need to get you some Bermuda shorts. I have two pairs, but they wouldn't be up to your standard. Let's get to the shop before it closes. Have you a decent shirt on the yacht? We need to try our best to fit in. It helps me with the spending parents."

"No, I don't have anything formal and neat, so I hope my credit card will work here. If not, can you sub me?"

"Depends what's in it for me."

"I'll buy you dinner at the uni café."

"Thanks a bunch. Let's go."

CHAPTER 37

Morning arrived, loaded with a mixture of excitement, anticipation, and relief. Ewan was curious about Tom's trip and wanted to re-live what he had been through, so the questions started. "How did you manage to navigate and sleep? And why did we lose track of you?"

"It wasn't a big deal. The yacht is stuffed with computery, and it was just a case of downloading the route and following the predicted plot. There's a triple-safe autopilot that I just had to watch, and if I nodded off, there was an ear-splitting warning klaxon to warn me if it sensed a problem. Sometimes it would just be a mismatch of co-ordinates, sometimes a big swell would cause the mechanics to over-compensate, but for the most part, it behaved. And I switched off the transponder when I thought my track would give the game away. You'd have seen that I was aiming for Bermuda, and the surprise element would have disappeared."

"Well, you almost disappeared under Ragged Rock. What would have happened if something had gone wrong earlier? Where would you've been then? At the bottom of the ocean and me best-friendless?"

"It was okay, I still had my Emergency Locator Beacon

that I could trigger at any time, and that's what I did when the rudder broke. Don't worry, I didn't and don't intend leaving you friendless."

"Okay, I won't go on. Suffice to say, I was bloody worried, and tried to contact Graham to see if he knew anything but couldn't get through."

"Gee, thanks for the concern; I'm truly sorry. I'll make it up to you somehow. We can talk about Graham later. There's quite a bit I want to go over with you."

"Right, let's get togged up for the barbeque."

As they walked into the Sailing Club lounge, Ewan nudged Tom. "I like your pink shorts and striped shirt. Do you think they fit in? It emphasises what a beautiful butt you have, and Bahamian pink is standard here. Just remember, we are only here for a barbeque. It's not a formal dinner. That said, you look stunning and very attractive to me."

"You know very well it was the only shorts that matched my inside leg; the others looked like jodhpurs, and if it does my butt credit, I can't help it. I'm made that way. And the striped shirt was in the uni's colours, so I feel secure. Let's aim for the bar; it looks like they have a huge punchbowl, and I'm ready to relax. If you see me sway too much, you can always rescue me again. And that poster on a race to the UK looks intriguing. What do you think?"

"Do you need any more pressure?"

"No, but I'm going that way anyway, so may as well try my hand at doing it. The prizes are unimportant; remember, it's the taking part, so they say. The boat should be ready to try out on Friday. Archie has done a brilliant job. How should I pay him?"

"I've taken care of that. All he wants is that you do

a press release at the sailing club on the Solent when you get back and mention his services after your exciting close call. Normally, all the posh ones go to the other boatyard here and don't know they are getting a crappy, rushed job. You can tilt the scales in his favour, and it will get up the nose of the opposition. And talking of noses, over there is a big florid one. Be nice to him. He's the Club president, and you'll need honorary membership from him to compete. Don't overdo the SA connection; saying you were escaping, which is true, will go down well. Just be your sweet and fawning self."

"I'm not great in conversation if I suspect it's money that talks. I decided to sell the SA consultancy business because I saw too much corruption and backhanders. Graham said it was the only way to do business, but I couldn't agree. I know Dad was asked to contribute to political funding, but he always said he wasn't going to give money to the lazy bastards who'd never done a full day's work in their life. I didn't tell you before, but there were some suspicious incidents that scared my mum. Several near accidents on the local roads couldn't all be coincidence. In the end, Dad hired security guards, but I wasn't sure if he was just paying for insurance that we shouldn't have needed. When I spoke to the chief detective on the burglary case, he said this was often done to pressure companies into paying 'safety' dues. In my opinion, the whole bloody place is corrupt. That's why giving the company to Graham removes pressure from myself and Sarah. Jerry, her husband, is safely installed as a first officer in British Airways; he has the escape mechanism. Now will this president guy expect me to grease his palm to enter the competition?"

"Look, he's stopped to glad-hand someone, but it looks like we're next. Remember, be tactful.

The florid nose approached. "Well, hello. It's good to see you again, Ewan. I hear that the rescue team was at its best."

Ewan smiled. "All in a day's work."

"And you must be Scarborough Fair," as he nodded towards Tom.

"I apologise for my untimely and disruptive arrival. If I can do anything to make amends, I am at your service."

"Not at all. We sailors have to look after each other. I hope Ewan has shown you our excellent hospitality."

"Oh, he has definitely done that," Tom responded with a sideways glance and a reassuring slow nod. "And thank you for inviting us to the barbeque. I hope to meet some of your club that can give me pointers on my next leg."

"No need for pointers. Please accept an invitation for our next race. It's to the UK, and you'll be in good company. We organise the race every year and have ironed out all the wrinkles except, of course, the weather. I'll get you installed as an honorary member so you can take part officially, and the Club facilities are at your disposal. What do you say?"

"I'd love to. There's always safety in numbers, and I would relish the challenge."

"Consider it done. Right, I must go and test that the punch is still up to standard. Good to meet you." And he was gone, with Ewan and Tom smirking at each other.

CHAPTER 38

Accepted for honorary membership of the yacht club, courtesy of "Florid Nose", the timing of the Bermuda-UK race gave them a month to prepare. The race would start off just in front of the hurricane season that the Bahamas had already witnessed, and Ewan would fly back at the end of the week to Heathrow. The intention was to meet again on the Solent and celebrate Tom's final homecoming. Meanwhile, they both fitted in a busy schedule of diving, boat prep, and rescue practice. And the practice turned real when a couple radioed for help with a flooded engine. Tom was first to board with Ewan again acting as linesman. The tow into the harbour was uneventful, and Ewan watched Tom use his charm to keep the couple and their attractive daughter amused.

Once on dry land, the couple expressed their thanks, and the daughter gave Tom a grateful hug. Ewan noticed it and laughed, raising his eyebrows in reply. The father also noticed and gave a small frown. Perhaps he thought his daughter was vulnerable to a knight on a white charger. He almost said so when they came back to the boat to pick up some possessions. Ewan, on the spur of the moment, started walking away with Tom, and took his hand. Ewan turned back to look at the father and saw him visibly relax. Ewan let Tom into the secret, and they both laughed. But Bermuda was not a place to be too public. It was a small but intimate moment to treasure. As they walked, Tom seemed ill at ease.

"Tom, what's up? You've gone very quiet. We still have five days to go. Are you having second thoughts?"

"No, but I still have to fill you in on SA."

"What exactly?"

"Well, I told you I've sold the consultancy, but I didn't mention Dad's yacht-building company in detail. It's not big, about thirty people, and they are the cream of the bunch. Dad knew who to pick, and they lead the field in SA. I've kept it running, despite me telling you I wanted to cut all ties with SA. The guy in charge is smart and streetwise. He built Dad's one, which is unlike any other class, and we've two boats well-on in build, and another has just had the keel laid, and a full order book. It was Dad's ambition to get a yacht class in his name, so these were being built to secure his reputation. I visited the factory to see the process. The build starts in a 3 D printed mould, which is a first in SA. The composite work is the latest in carbon fibre with a secret system of reinforcing carbon bars. Knowing the construction process should help with the uni project. I'm sure we can get them to review our plans and maybe even make a model. Look, here are some photos on my laptop to kindle your interest."

"Very impressive. The sale price must be astronomical. Who can afford it?"

"You would be surprised at the 'I want one brigade'. They need places to park their money, and it gives them bragging rights. By me bringing back the prototype to the UK, it should turn heads and is cheap but effective publicity. What do you think?"

"Look, I'm too green in the sailing fraternity to offer an opinion, but if it makes you happy, I'm all for it."

"I sounded Sarah out, and she thought it was good to keep Dad's memory alive. The team are pretty savvy, know the score, and work to strict budgets, and it also makes a healthy profit. The company is too small to be attractive to the mafia, and I can trust the team to keep everything clean. At some stage, a move to the UK could be possible, and Southampton would make an attractive base if the design wins approval. Would that interest you?"

"You bet. It sounds exciting. Once uni is out of the way, anything is possible, as long as it doesn't put you under too much strain."

"Don't worry, I'm beginning to relax more. I call it the 'Ewan effect'. Let's go see Archie. He promised to take us out on the rigid inflatable boat; I think he called it a RIB and said something about a recce."

They arrived at the jetty, and Archie was already on the RIB with the engine running. The word that went around was that the RIB had just had its annual overhaul and needed the test. It was a cover for Tom to learn the local currents that the club members already thought they knew, and would have given them a head start. But there were currents that only Archie knew. As they re-entered the harbour, Ewan suggested they go to the office to consult the charts. "I've beat you to it. The missus is waiting for us, and you probably don't know, but she was an Olympic sailor in her day. She has brought her old Atlantic competition paperwork. She wants to share some secrets, and, Tom, you'll be surprised what she can tell you."

Ewan looked at Tom and nodded vigorously. "That sounds great. Tom needs all the help he can get, and I'm useless as a source of knowledge, being the novice that I am."

As they entered the office, Archie's missus, a buxom woman with long bleached hair and a well-worn face, was at the chart table, which sported a tartan tablecloth, a huge pot of tea, and a mound of shortbread. Ewan beamed at her. She had kept Ewan supplied with late dinner meals when the klaxon had made it a long day. "Hello, Mrs MacKay. I must thank you for those delicious Scottish meals. I think I put some weight on."

"No problem; glad to reward your dedication, and please call me Brenda."

"This is Tom, my sailing partner. He was a lost stray. I… I mean we, picked him off Devil's Rock. Now he wants to beat his sea demons, but we need to increase his odds of survival. Archie says you have secrets that might help."

"Right, start with the shortbread and all will be revealed." She had pinned a chart to the navigation board.

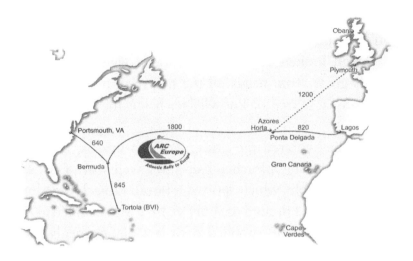

"Well, I've raced many times up and down the Atlantic and across and back to the UK, with some success." Archie laughed out loud. "Ignore him," Brenda said. "I've looked out my old winning routes. Have a look. You need to remember that the later in the year you leave here, the more influence you will get from the Gulf Stream flows. I've downloaded an official app that we use here for the ARC Europe race. It's here on the computer." Tom was all agog, and turned to Ewan sporting a very wide grin and eyebrows doing a double take in astonishment.

"That looks amazing and, I must say, totally unexpected. I'm happy to pay for the app, and I have quite a bit of electronic wizardry to establish an uplink. You can be my secret weapon."

"I'm not sure about that, but it's state of the art and free to us here as we host some of the races, so it's gratis to you." Tom's smile grew even wider. "It has an automatic metrological feed, so as long as you get the satellite link, you'll know what's ahead and around you. Mind you, you can't beat a chart and a biro, so we'll get this one printed out. It's also on this storage stick that can go straight into your laptop. I've chosen a more northerly route than you might expect. It's normal for the single-handed boats to follow a southerly route and go via Horta in the Azores. Archie tells me you want to sail in Group Two, which is direct to the UK. You'll get more speed further north, but it may get a bit lumpy. Have a look, and we can do a thorough route plan this evening if it's all right with you; bring your laptop. And I'm making fish and chips so you both had better be hungry." With much grinning and profuse thanks, they left the office on a high. Once back at the container, they both decided on a quick nap together. It was a warm fuzzy feeling for both of them, probably to prepare for their impending separation.

Brenda's dinner was a veritable feast. Their appetites had grown with the sea air, but it was still difficult to do justice to the pile of food she had prepared. Then they talked shop, with Ewan learning more about depressions and cavorting frontal systems than he would ever get from pottering about on the Solent. "Brenda, what is the best tip you could give Tom that might get him ahead of the competition?" Ewan asked with his most ingratiating smile.

"Right. For a start, you need the right sails at the right time. Not when you get overtaken by the weather. You might lose a little time waiting for a front to overtake you, but you need to catch and ride the prevailing westerly favourable winds when they are given to you. Your barometer tells you what is happening where you are. The satellite download will tell you what's around you. My punt is to go north-east till you get to 40 North, enter the Gulf Stream before 50

West, then dig into the current. Don't be afraid to rig your sails for stormy weather and stay with the flow. Even be prepared to go further north if the sails will take it. After all, you are in a competition."

Before Tom could reply, Ewan chirped up. "But Tom needs to de-risk as he is single-handed, doesn't he?"

"With what I've seen of all the aids on *Scarborough Fair*, and its build, and Tom fit and well, the boat can take the strain."

"But what happens if the rudder packs in again?"

From his seat on the couch, Archie intervened. "The boat has bow and stern thrusters as a back-up. The reason Tom couldn't use them before was because some idiot in Rio removed the in-line fuses during the engine upgrade and forgot to replace them. There are now spare fuses in the overhead locker. Next question."

"Okay, I was only just saying ..." They all looked at a crest-fallen Ewan and laughed. It was getting late. "Thanks, Brenda, for a superb dinner and my navigation teach-in. I only hope Tom was paying attention. How can we repay you?"

"All I want Tom to do is beat Florid Nose – I think that's what you called him – to the finishing line. That will be my reward. I'll keep my beady eye on progress." It was a brilliant evening with good food, good company, and precious insights to the sailing plan.

The Departure day arrived in a rush. Archie took them both through all the work he had done, and prep work on the engine and innards.

"Tom, let's do a last check on the boat. I want to make sure you don't have to divert en route."

They entered the cockpit, and Tom kept up a running

commentary of the preparation. "Look, the fuel had been topped up, and all the batteries are all fully charged; here are the voltage gauges, and look, here are the spare thruster fuses. Both GPSs check out, and say we are in Bermuda – that's a good start. The toilet is pristine, but I don't know for how long; peeing at an angle is an art I haven't quite mastered. Thanks for packing all my belongings in the cupboards; it makes me feel good. And the crucial pills are in three different places, so always accessible. Here's the route pinned to the chart board." Ewan noticed his photo was still in place. "The gun's due to sound at noon, and we're done in here, so why don't we spend the rest of the morning walking hand-in-hand and talking? I need to imprint some stuff into my memory banks. And here's a hug for starters."

They sat down on a bench at the top of Lighthouse Hill overlooking the harbour with the light pulsing its triple-flash even in daylight; it was a magnificent view, with the sea a dazzling azure blue. The surrounding houses were the posh, white, expensive, square boxes with their railed terraces sparkling in the sun; the container put up a brave show of being one of them. They could make out *Scarborough Fair* with the stern and mooring lines tying it firmly to the dock, where Ewan would have liked it to remain. Leaning into one another, they enjoyed the closeness, but neither mentioned how much they were going to miss such closeness.

"Tom, you need to be bloody careful on the water. I am scared for you, and if I'm honest, scared for both of us. You can't imagine what I went through when I lost contact with you before. I don't want to go through that again. I have a feeling for you that's difficult to describe. I know it's love, but that doesn't even begin to cover it. I would be lost now without you, and our second year at uni, together, is my future, our future. I only hope you feel the same."

"Just look into my eyes. What do you see?"

"The same bloody eyes that caught me before."

"Well, they've caught you again, and forever. Please never doubt that. Absence makes the heart grow fonder, and that's exactly what happened when the rudder broke. I could only think of you, and that's what kept me going. We have something people talk about as precious and can't be bought or traded. My head is full of you, and I like the feeling. And your lips look bloody inviting. Come closer."

Their goodbyes were said in private, so at the dockside no one could tell how much they felt for each other; it was a brilliant secret that kept giving. Ewan elected to watch from Spy Hill to allow Tom to concentrate on getting underway. He was full of emotion and excited for Tom, who was fulfilling a mission he had set himself. The gun sounded, and it took Ewan's heart by surprise. The armada entered the exit channel abeam Puget Island. It was a strange feeling to see the yachts start to beat against the currents, knowing that Tom was in their midst. He lost sight of the sail as the haze swallowed Tom's yacht. It would take Tom about three weeks to cover the three thousand miles to Southampton.

Without Tom, the week went slowly, despite Ewan working all the hours available. He started wrapping up for his departure, and Uncle Bert kept adding to his load, to get his money's worth. Archie sensed the change in Ewan's mood, and insisted the nightly pub visit was essential practice. Ewan hinted that Tom was more than just a good friend, but he never reached disclosure. Staid Bermuda was not a place for confessions, and Uncle Bert was of the old school.

CHAPTER 39

Archie drove Ewan to the airport with plenty of time to spare. It was a strange feeling to be leaving a fun routine and his container home. Ewan promised Uncle Bert that he would be back next year, and said a coat of paint wouldn't go amiss on the "house". The cheque was given grudgingly, and Ewan made sure it was signed and in-date. But they had shaken hands warmly.

Ewan was about to get out of the Jeep, when Archie spoke. "Look, you've been a great asset; you take the heat off me when you're here. As a thanks to you, I've let Tom into a secret. The route we recce'd with the RIB is unpublished. There's a promontory that, with a westerly wind, delivers a strong current to the north-east for a long time, but the area is quite shallow. I discussed it with Tom and, using his echo-sounder and my print-out, I saw he made it into that flow to his advantage; the others think they knew the shallows, but I know them better. It's a thanks for all your help, and you now know the secret as well. It's given him a good lead at the moment. Have a safe journey." With a quick firm handshake, he was gone, and Ewan slowly walked into the terminal building, thinking that life could always throw up surprises.

Finally getting to the front of the queue, Ewan offered a copy of his booking, only to be told he was in the wrong queue. Well, the sign said BA 111 to London Heathrow. The check-in girl pointed down the concourse to another desk. Again, Ewan gave his docs. On checking his paperwork, the girl pointed to the last desk in the row. It said, "First Class Only", and he knew there must be something wrong. There was no queue, so he offered his paperwork again, and was given a huge smile. "Welcome, Mr Murray. I've just checked you in. You have seat 1A. Have you used the lounge before?" Ewan shook his head, and instantly a figure appeared alongside and said, "Follow me, please, sir." In a bit of a daze, it dawned on Ewan that when Tom printed out his itinerary, he must have arranged secretly for an upgrade. Ewan couldn't help smiling. The ticket must have cost the equivalent of a year's supply of crisps.

CHAPTER 40

It wasn't just a seat. It was a luxury suite with all manner of gadgets, and the aircraft was the BOAC painted 747. Ewan took lots of photos to show Tom.

Champagne was brought by a smiling, motherly-looking attendant. She suggested that once he had settled down, he should have a look at the menu and choose his first wine. He felt he was in an expensive cocoon.

The journey was a mixture of eating, cloud-watching, and self-pinching. He thought he could get used to this type of luxury that Tom probably found normal. He would take Tom to task on the cost of the indulgence.

The seat had a computer power supply, so Ewan retrieved his laptop from his carry-on. Stuck to the inside flap was an envelope with his name on it. With shaking fingers, Ewan opened the envelope to find a picture of a naked Tom standing in the yacht's cabin with Ewan's photo in the background on the pin-board. A Post-it note said, "What you see is what you get – a selfie taken on the high seas – do you miss me?" Ewan's grin almost hurt him. At least in first class, no one could see the revelation or Ewan's expression. It was as uplifting as life could get. Apart, that is, from remembering that as dinner was served, Tom was thirty thousand feet below just entering the Gulf Stream current, on his own. The fact pulled at Ewan's heart. The rest of the journey was total cloud nine.

CHAPTER 41

Ewan busied himself to fend off the flat's loneliness, but there was only so much cleaning he could do. Study and meeting with the team filled the void. There was two weeks before Tom's scheduled arrival. Fred had sent copious data on their project, so digesting it was a huge task. Somehow, Fred had included a selfie at his computer. His face was full of concentration, and he looked just as handsome with dangling blonde hair. The photo tugged at Ewan's heartstrings, but he knew there was nothing he could do.

The team began developing their next presentation and still sailed at the weekend on the Solent to revitalise their connection. It was a strange feeling to be on the water at the same time as Tom, but the Solent proved no contest. Ewan brought them up to date with Tom's escapades, but left out any hint of their relationship. There would be a time and place for that, when they would both be relaxed enough to face the truth.

Tom's progress was available on the race website, and, though not in the lead, it was going to be a close-run thing. Some of the entrants had attempted the race before, and reading previous reports, it seemed the Bay of Biscay was the sticking point for many a leader, but Tom was on a much more northerly track and possibly sitting in the Western Atlantic current. Ewan saw that by the end of the second week, Tom had gone above 45 North. He had said he was only going to use the weather prediction download as guide; they had discussed it, and Brenda had wanted Tom to plot his course using intuition and the signs around him. He would learn what worked and what didn't, and get a better feeling for the currents. She said the boat always gave good feedback and shouldn't be ignored. Ewan wanted a more academic approach, but lost the argument. Ewan thought Brenda must have had a secret talk with Tom, because they had never even hinted about going that far north. Remembering her Olympic medals, Ewan guessed she was even smarter than Archie gave her credit. She had mentioned that one of her best transits had been just south of the iceberg tracks abeam Newfoundland. Maybe Tom was doing the same. The debrief in Southampton would be instructive, truthful, and revealing.

CHAPTER 42

The day prior to hitting the South West Approaches and the Channel, Ewan was following Tom's track, which was definitely much further north than the others. It looked like the President's yacht was in the lead with Tom challenging for a place in the top four. Ignoring the weather predictions had been a gamble, but Tom said he felt he had nothing to lose or prove except be true to Brenda's intuition. Tom's read-out was showing twenty knots, which was either a faulty indication or Tom was being pulled by a spinnaker, which he couldn't be. He was probably rigged for a storm-force wind and an almighty ocean hand was moving him at a stupendous pace: good old Brenda.

A meeting with the rest of the team at tea-time in the flat proved to be a boisterous affair, and Claire was, abnormally, just as excited. They split for the evening, and Ewan was left to pace the flat in a buoyant mood, probably to match the buoyant on-wave performance of Tom. Ewan planned to get to the finish line at the Royal Yacht Club moorings an hour early. He went to bed, but sleep didn't come easily. Some dream of shipwrecks and dismasted schooners fought with unknown sea-creatures that Ewan woke in a sweat, and it was only two a.m. The morning didn't get any better as a mixture of fear and anticipation kept sleep at bay.

CHAPTER 43

The alarm went off, and Ewan woke with a jolt, feeling he had only just gone off to sleep. But he felt excited with an unusually rapid heartbeat. Showered and dressed, Ewan skipped breakfast. His tum was doing somersaults. A cooling-off cycle ride was no help, so he arrived at the finish point of the race very early. It was an unusually bright day after a bleak week, and the Solent sparkled. The snobbish sailing club buildings were bedecked with bunting, and lots of fashionably well-dressed enthusiasts were mingling on the club lawn. Access was limited to members, so Ewan stood by the fence to drink in the atmosphere, understanding that they didn't know he had a mate skippering one of the competing boats - and he was a very, very close mate.

An air of anticipation was fostered by a loudspeaker giving the distance of the leading boat without giving its name. But who won wasn't important to Ewan. He just wanted Tom back to him in one piece. The minutes ticked by very slowly – too slowly. There was sufficient wind to give the boats traction, but the Solent was notorious with its counter currents. Suddenly a large outdoor screen lit up and gave a view down river. A couple of sails were just visible in the distance. Ewan fingered the chain round his neck.

A commentator started up, but the wind stole his voice. The boat-hulls became distinctive, and Ewan could swear one of them was Tom's. He moved his position to stand under one of the speakers to hear the name *Bermuda Star* and then *Scarborough Fair*. It was going to be a close-run thing. Then one of the boats went about and for a moment its sail seemed to get caught on the water. The other boat stayed on the same tack and visibly moved ahead. The next thing Ewan knew was that the finish gun went off, and *Scarborough Fair* was announced as the winner. Ewan's chest puffed out, and he punched the air. The screen showed the boat arriving and being tied up at the jetty. The next time Ewan looked, there was Tom on deck being hugged by a girl, and Tom was carrying a baby. Ewan stood in shock, and remained in the alleyway that led to the moorings.

Ewan couldn't move; his mind was racing. He'd witnessed something that he couldn't explain. Tom had been secretive at times, but – a baby? When could the child have been conceived in SA? And who was the girl? Ewan's despair made his tum do more somersaults. Is Tom married? It's not his sister. What a fool he had been. Should he back out and retreat to the flat? Did that torn photo have a deeper meaning?

He was about to leave when Tom, the girl, and the baby came round the corner. Tom shouted, came forward, and grabbed Ewan. By this time Ewan was bright red, and there was no place to hide.

"Meet two of the loves of my life. What do you think of him, Ewan? See this little chap with the curly hair? Does he have my eyes and hair?"

"Well ..." A male arrived, puffing.

"Okay, I can take him now. I've disposed of the nappy." Ewan's confusion was evident to all.

"Ewan, let me introduce my cousin Stan, his wife Doreen, and my nephew, Noah." Tom eyed Ewan and concluded what Ewan was thinking. "You didn't, did you?"

"What?"

"Think I got married in SA and had a baby?"

"Of course not." But his scarlet face said it all. The rings on the chain round his neck were pressing on his throat.

"Come see the yacht and my confined quarters for most of the last month." They trooped on board as Tom batted off the security guards. Tom went first with Ewan stepping gingerly in his non-deck shoes. Tom was waiting at the bottom of the stairs with his arms outstretched. As Ewan arrived on the last step, the boat was hit by some wash and he fell forward; they collided. "What are these?" Tom asked, fingering rings that had popped out from around Ewan's neck.

"Oh, just a couple of rings."

"Oh yeah. Let me see." Tom stood behind Ewan and undid the gold chain. The yacht moved under the wash of a passing vessel, and they came together, and some spark happened that gave Ewan goose bumps. Tom examined the rings and saw anchors etched on them.

"They're not precious," Ewan said ruefully. "Just signet rings from your broken rudder fixings. Archie made them for me as keepsakes." Tom held the rings to the light and noticed etchings inside both. Two sets of initials either side of a heart.

"Signet rings you say," Tom muttered with an incredulous look.

"Yup."

"But they have our initials inside."

"Do they really?" Ewan said, grinning. " I had the local jeweller engrave them in secret, so Archie wouldn't know." Tom took one, pulled Ewan's hand towards him and placed it on the third finger of Ewan's left hand. They both beamed.

"Now it's your turn."

"Which finger again?"

"This one, dummy."

"Done."

"I take it we are a certified item?"

"Yup, again. But you said you had something to show me."

"It's been overtaken by events, but here it is. It's the selfie we took in the rigging of that tall yacht knowing nobody would see us kissing. I was going to use it to say something important, but the rings have already said it."

"What are you two up to?" came a voice from the deck. "We're here to get the celebrations underway."

"Come down," Tom shouted. "I've had enough 'underway' to last me a lifetime, but we have another reason for a celebration. We've something to show you, and I'm about to open the champagne." As Doreen and Stan with the baby reached the bottom of the stairs, they were confronted by Tom and Ewan holding hands. "Ewan, do you want to?"

"No, you do it, you're so better with words than I am."

"Well, we just got engaged, despite Ewan's worst fears."

"To whom?" they asked in unison.

"Each other, of course." Tom uncorked the champagne,

and the baby cried at the pop. "My toast. To my homecoming after a long voyage of realisation, but more importantly, my engagement to someone who previously was my best friend."

CHAPTER 44

"Tom, stop pushing. I've got to get the key in the lock."

"Hurry up. I need to get inside and feel secure with the floor not moving. That was quite an ending."

"For you and me both. They're quite a snooty bunch at the club, and those security guys kept looking down their noses at me. I obviously didn't fit in or match their posh clientele image. I had to hold my tongue. Right, we're in. I hope the flat is clean enough for you. I almost wore out a pair of marigolds."

"Come here. This is what I've been dreaming of."

"Me too. Golly, you've got hair on your chin again. I think you've lost weight. My arms go round you all the way plus a bit."

"I was pining for you. Now I can relax, eat, and sleep, but I'm not sure of the order."

"Look, have a lie down and when you feel hungry, I'll break out the designer sandwiches, and, before you ask, they're not from the uni canteen." Tom's phone rang continuously, but they agreed today was theirs alone. Tomorrow, the outside world could become involved.

"That was hard work getting into the marina this morning. I know we're only visitors, but he hadn't even heard of the competition or *Scarborough Fair* from yesterday, despite my trying to sing it to him. I don't think he was amused. Obviously, the office knew, but said we can't have the gate code. They all seem quite a stuck-up bunch, trying to be so exclusive. Right, I'll go first as I still have my sea-legs." The boat looked the part as it swayed on the water with the sun bouncing off the stainless steel. "I think we have a message." Stuck to the cabin door was an envelope. Tom opened it. "Bloody hell, they've given us notice to move off the mooring in four days' time. That's nice and friendly. I'll talk to our sailing club; I know they'll accommodate us, and I'll put a word in about this lot here, but not before I've spoken to that obnoxious secretary who met me and thought I wasn't dressed properly to accept the Challenge Cup. He was definitely up his own arse, and his moustache needed cleaning to get rid of the smell obviously emanating from his personal closeness to his curry lunch. Let's pay him a visit to see what we need to do to get membership."

As they entered the central hall of the club, the receptionist looked up, smiling. Ewan thought that was a good sign, until Tom asked to see the club secretary, when she gave a grimace, and asked what it was about. "How do we apply for membership?" Tom replied, trying a disarming smile.

Her reply was evasive with lots of shrugs and nods. "Well, there is a waiting list, but it's measured in years, and you have to be recommended by two existing members." She dropped her voice, looked towards the secretary's door, then whispered, "That's unless you became a gold member, a very expensive option, and it seems only Russians can afford it these days."

"Well do you have a figure I can work to so I can approach the Secretary?"

"I don't have a figure, but, oops, here he comes. Mr Urquhart, these gentlemen were enquiring about membership."

"I'm afraid all approaches must be in writing, and the committee are quite exact in the standards they demand of members." He was looking them both up and down, and his pinstriped suit and half-moon glasses gave him the air of a headmaster.

"That's good to know," Tom said in his poshest voice. I'll get my staff to pen something."

"Oh, there is a long waiting list, and any craft anchored here has to meet rigorous criteria."

"Well, we arrived from Bermuda in yesterday's competition, so our yacht must be up to scratch. What did bother us was the note on the cabin door giving us four days' notice to move. I think you signed the letter."

"That's normal practice here as we would be inundated with all sorts."

"Well, ours is definitely not an 'all sorts'. I trust you'll remember our conversation when you learn of the new Yorkshire fifty-foot class soon to be unveiled by *Sailing World*. You will have just hosted the first one. I think we'll leave you with that thought. Let's go, Ewan." They gave a nod to the receptionist on the way out, and she couldn't hide her smirk.

CHAPTER 46

They were in the cabin giving *Scarborough Fair* a thorough clean when Tom's phone pinged. "Ewan, can you grab it, I've got my marigolds on."

"Sure. It looks like an international call. Does Philip ring a bell, pardon the pun?"

"He's our lawyer in SA. I'd better take it." Tom answered the call with occasional grunts. He put the phone down looking glum. "I've just been told that the trial will take place in Cape Town starting in early-December. I said I want to be there. He also mentioned that there have been overtures, or you could say threats, to Yorkshire Yachts, coming from some local kingpin. He reckons it's about drugs and drug-running using yachts. I was warned about that in Rio. They build the drugs into the yacht or stick the drugs under the hull. I wondered why the Rio sailing club insisted a diver check the boat before I left. I've said it before, SA is dodgy."

"Archie said it was standard procedure in Bermuda to check inbound yachts for contraband, and he mentioned they pulled about one a week in the busy season. You wouldn't have noticed the sniffer dog giving yours a once-over after you docked because we were on our way to get you fixed. It was a good job you were clean."

"I think I was too far gone to care, if you remember, though I did have a fair stash of anti-malaria tablets. Now, from what the lawyer said, I'm beginning to feel uneasy about what could happen to the company in SA. It would make sense to be there and discuss our options. What do you think? You know I've spoken before about moving the whole organisation to the UK. Maybe that idea can't wait."

"I know the trial will be tough on you, but it should make closure easier, so attending is a good idea, and it should be your first priority. If Sarah is going to be there, she'll need you. And you talked about emptying the house and disposing of the contents. That's a huge task, and she may want an input. Sorting out what you want to do with the company will fill any spare time you have, and you may even need longer. Normally, uni will give you an extra couple of weeks if it's an emergency. You can always bounce any ideas off me as I guard the flat. I can ask the stupid questions that no one else will ask. You'll need to prime the critical people before you get there so they can do their own homework. I guess your accountant and lawyer are top of the list. Will Graham be able to help?"

"Absolutely. He knows all about Dad's affairs and has already made suggestions and is sorting out all the finances for me; he's in touch with Norm, Dad's accountant in the UK. I still have to unlock the safe in the house. The detective in charge hinted that my parents were likely shot because he wouldn't reveal where it was. Dad always said that what he had was earned, not pilfered or embezzled. He was proud of that and knew many around him who weren't clean. Philip said the balance sheet is very strong, meaning the sums are expected to be bloody huge. Dad was no slouch at investing. Even Broadview will fetch a good price for Sarah, and there are the precious antiques which he loved collecting; they need to be sold. She has let me know that she doesn't want reminders of the past; I feel the same, and the house now has too much sadness, too much horror, for both of us to be comfortable using it."

"Well, when it happened to me, I needed the security of home, but my parents' bedroom was a no-go area for me, and Aunt Bessie had to dispose of all my parents' clothes; I was too young to get involved. Eventually, the kitchen and sitting room started to bring back too many memories, and I was glad when I moved. You probably feel the same about Broadview."

"I do. As soon as we've moved all the stuff, it will go on the market "

"Why don't we prepare a list of questions you need to ask on arrival? As regards the future of the Yorkshire Yachts, you might even want to talk through possible scenarios with your tutor. If he's on board, it should help with your thesis structure, and you can cover all the compulsory term headings from finance all the way to legal, plus an international twist if you factor in the mafia angle as well; just call it 'security aspects'. It would be interesting to make the examiners feel uncomfortable."

"Good idea. That all makes sense."

"If you leave at the end of term when we break up for the hols, it'll give you a full month there, and that could be enough time to get the company protected. Plus, it would be great for you to see your new nephew, wouldn't it?"

"You're right. Look, I know this might sound too big

an ask, but why don't you come with me to SA for the holiday period? You would be ideal company and could give me oodles of common sense, and the weather is great for sailing. I'm sure Eric would be happy to guard the flat here, provided we stock the wine cellar. Before you answer, I want you on the company payroll as a partner, which makes talking about us easier. It'll shut up the local relations, and we won't have to pretend, and you won't have to get anxious about expenses. There is a mountain of money, and I would feel a damn sight safer with you."

"I'm not sure about the last bit, but if I can help, of course I will. I don't know how Scotland will take my absence, but, when I think about it, that time of year always brings back bad memories. As long as I can do some distance learning with Fred, he'll probably be just as happy as if I was there. It'll be interesting to celebrate Hogmanay in a strange country. I must say, the bit about drugs sounds ominous."

"Brilliant, I owe you. These rings work wonders. You've just lifted a great weight off my shoulders, and I really want you to meet Sarah; remember, she doesn't know about us yet. I think the drugs issue is best handled by the lawyer's contacts; he says he has plenty, so we will be well protected and in good, big hands."

CHAPTER 47

The end-of-term celebrations were muted. The team knew that Tom had the trial ahead, though they didn't know of the other potential trouble in Cape Town. Ewan made Tom stick to their study timetable, and filled the time in between with squash and sailing. It was a sort of space-filling therapy to avoid talking about the monster in the room, the impending court appearance. Tom shared all the lawyer bumpf with Ewan, and they spent many hours evolving a possible plan to repatriate Yorkshire Yachts to Southampton. Ewan had encouraged Tom to propose the repatriation scenario to his tutor as his second-year project, but, as yet, there hadn't been any feedback. "Tom, we spoke about bringing your tutor on board. Any news?"

"Sorry. With everything going on, I forgot to tell you. I did speak to him, and he was all for it. He liked the idea of the relocation of a going concern as a proper second year topic. He agreed that, suitably argued with full supporting evidence, it should provide a good basis for a thesis, provided the company name was disguised. Thanks for that, I owe you one."

"Don't mention it. I'm full of bright ideas that don't normally see the light of day. Let's go and do the duty clean of the bulwarks." Ewan's eyes sparkled and he grinned. "I like saying that word."

With the yacht accepted at the school marina, Tom and Ewan earned plenty of kudos owning such a prestigious boat. There was a continuous stream of gawking visitors, but it was good publicity for what Tom hoped would be a new class of yacht. Eric and Claire were thrilled to be part of it, and Claire decided to arrange for them all to have T-shirts. Choosing the design and colours led to many accusations of male chauvinism, and pink was definitely excluded from the options. They settled on different shades of purple and blue, with Claire as the only dissenting voice.

Ewan and Tom cycled around the area looking for potential sites that might offer a home for Yorkshire Yachts, an echo of Ewan's recce trips when he first arrived. Facilities at various harbours made them feel positive, and it was proving to be an exciting challenge. The old slipways of the flying boats were everywhere and proved a magnet for their imaginations. The Ocean Terminal with its museum was a huge visitor attraction and even had a Sunderland flying boat as a gate guardian to emphasise its heritage. They asked a few estate agents what commercial properties were available, but the staff were very off-hand with what they assumed were timewasters and not two young potential buyers; it was as if they needed to see the colour of Tom's money. He said as much to one toffee-nosed suited gent.

Although Ewan kept regular computer contact with Fred on their project, he also spoke on the phone to Fred's mum every so often to let her know what they were doing. She said it had proved a lifeline for Fred who believed his research made a vital contribution to the boat-plane. Ewan assured her that it did, and that they were agog at his logical and methodical approach, something the team were not at all good at. He explained to her that it was difficult to tell Fred how much he was appreciated, but Mrs Oliphant just asked to include him whenever they could; it gave his energy a brilliant outlet. On one of the exchanges with Fred about the floatplane location, one response took them completely by surprise. Fred, with his meticulous research on a possible base, launch facilities, and hangarage, unearthed a ramp and warehouse for sale next to the snooty sailing club. Neither Tom nor Ewan had seen the almost derelict site as it had been hidden behind the club's enormous "KEEP-OUT" fencing. They were both astonished at the detail Fred had provided. It was currently in use for car storage. The footprint of the old floatplane berth included a ramp and a substantial warehouse with hardstanding and appeared to cover the access road and car park of the sailing club. It looked like the sailing club may have exercised squatters' rights over their access and car park. On relaying this to Fred, his response was adamant that the car park and access road were only listed three years prior, when the previous access road was demolished to make way for a club house extension, as per the local planning applications. Ewan and Tom were speechless. This was potential for a blockbuster moment of retribution, courtesy of Fred.

CHAPTER 48

The protective cocoon of first class evaporated as they touched down in Cape Town. Ewan felt the weight of the moment and tried to distract Tom from the looming trial by discussing the work they needed to complete as soon as they arrived. It was a strange meeting as they entered the arrival hall. Tom had spotted his sister straightaway, and Ewan didn't know what he should do or say. Sarah hugged Tom and gave him the baby. Tom grinned from ear to ear, making cooing noises that they all laughed at. Sarah then introduced Tom to Jerry. Ewan held back feeling uneasy and an intruder, but Tom grabbed Ewan and pushed him towards them. Sarah stepped forward and gave Ewan a hug, which he wasn't expecting, and Jerry grabbed him as if he were a long lost relative. They were all smiling, and the welcome felt genuine.

"This is Ewan, my best friend, and, to clear the air, we're engaged." Ewan received another hug from Sarah. Her eyes were sparkling, and she was nodding.

"That's perfect. I thought as much. Ewan, since you arrived at uni, Tom has not shut up about you, and I can see why. I'm so relieved, and thankful that you can beat him at squash." They laughed. "Let's get to Vineyard House and check the cellar. You won't be disappointed, I promise. The car and driver are waiting."

On arrival, Ewan noticed the guards at the estate entrance, and as they approached along an impressive drive, there were cameras at every bend. The house itself was a long low white building with carved arches. Vine rows stretched in all directions. As he entered the hallway, Ewan started to relax. Tom led the way, but Ewan was surprised at what he presumed were household staff carrying his luggage. It gave him an uncomfortable feeling, and he nudged Tom and frowned. Tom made calming gestures.

On their own in a very spacious bedroom, they hugged and sat on the bed. "Well, here we are, and I'm so bloody glad you agreed to come. If I appear down, I'm not. I'm with you."

"Look Tom, I have a great feeling we can get through this together. Sarah whispered to me that I'm her godsend. I don't know about that, but once we get the trial over, we can tackle everything and anything else."

"Philip said we can expect a call in the next few days for the trial start. Meanwhile, I want to take you sightseeing, and Sarah and Jerry want to escort you as well. You might become quite popular, even family."

"I hope I'm already popular with you."

"How's this for proof?"

CHAPTER 49

The call was expected but unwanted. Philip then emailed all the information about the court attendance. The security detail would pick them up from Vineyard House and deposit them at ten a.m. at the courthouse.

Ewan stepped out of the car to see a huge reddish-granite building, declaring itself the Western Cape Court House, and underneath it said "Hooggeregshof", the Afrikaans word meaning "supreme court". The impressive and tall colonnaded front boasted four Doric columns with a massive door to match - definitely a no-nonsense outfit.

They were ushered into a waiting room. Sarah had come on her own, with Jerry staying at home to be childminder, though they talked often on the phone. Ewan noticed that much of their exchange was in "security speak". It was a chilling thought that this must be their norm.

Tom introduced the prosecution counsel, a woman lawyer dressed in black robes with a white, what looked like, two-pronged tie. A search on his phone revealed that it was called a jabot, or in slang, a neck doily, that served no useful purpose other than to catch the ketchup from a hamburger. He mentioned this to Tom, but they all heard it and laughed. To Ewan, it seemed an oddly friendly atmosphere in such forbidding criminal surroundings. With security passes dangling from their necks, they were led into the court itself. Everywhere was a forest of dark mahogany. It resembled a theatre, and the gallery had a large balustrade with a sturdy brass rail. Above that was a massive dome filled with bright neon lights. Ewan thought it more severe and imposing than the one he remembered from a long time ago, which was now only a fleeting dark cloud. A maze of wooden chest-high panels made compartments everywhere. In the centre was the dock with steps leading up from below via a barred gate. Along the dock wall at intervals were large black numbers on a white background, one to three. To the right was the witness box, surrounded by lots of desks and bewigged barristers. In its lofty position, Ewan could just make out the ornate chair of the judge, and below to his left were the jury seats. Only the judge's seat was red; the others were varying shades of green. A thought crept from the recesses of his memory: at least no embarrassing plastic covers here.

No sooner had they sat down when the call was made, "All rise." As they stood up, the bowing started. Ewan just stared at the floor and tried to make himself as small as possible. Sarah was bracketed by Tom and himself. Their ordeal was only just beginning.

CHAPTER 50

They were seated as usual in the well of the court. Today was the last act of the proceedings. The previous days had been none too gentle on graphic detail and proved an ordeal for them all. When the three familiar figures of the accused were marched in, Ewan's eyes were drawn to the various tattoos visible on their exposed skin. These displayed their gang affiliations, he'd been told. They had an air of menace and anger about them. Although Tom had seen their mugshots in the local papers, in person they looked and acted boastful and treated the proceedings as a huge joke. They shrugged their shoulders when some detail of their actions was laboured by the prosecuting barrister. They were show-offs who didn't appear to have any scruples about their crimes or the devastation they had on the lives of those they robbed, maimed or killed. Tom whispered to Ewan behind Sarah's back. "Their behaviour sickens me. I would love to take out a gun and shoot them, and it would still be too good a result. They'll never know the pain they have caused Sarah and me."

"It's okay, Tom. You're shaking. Take some deep breaths."

"I feel sick. I just can't seem to get the picture of our dogs out of my mind." Sarah put an arm round Tom's shoulders and the moment passed. They were back in the present with noise coming from the dock.

The tallest of the three, the leader it transpired, kept tossing his dangling dreadlocks in the air and was muttering to himself. The other two had tightly woven patterns on their heads, and played to the gallery, which was now full of noisy friends and families. The women wore a variety of bright orange and green dresses with what appeared to Ewan to be bird's nests or fruit bowls on their heads. Their native garb definitely outshone the barristers and clerks and added an incongruous party-like atmosphere to the proceedings.

The three prisoners began to talk loudly to one another and shouted to their families. The judge banged his gavel and called for silence. A bunch of security guards spread among them and used their batons as cattle-prods to get silence.

The accused were told to stand. The court usher rose and faced the foreman of the jury. "Have you reached a verdict?"

"We have, and it is the verdict of us all."

"Do you find defendant number one guilty or not guilty?"

"Guilty." The prisoner turned to face the gallery and started shouting obscenities in Afrikaans. His grimace showed a vault of gold teeth, as ugly as it was repulsive. The crowd reacted with a roar, and the judge banged his gavel and threatened to clear the gallery. He knew Afrikaans and let the prisoner know it.

"Do you find defendant number two guilty or not guilty?"

"Guilty." There was a muted murmur from the gallery. This time the massively tattooed individual tore open his shirt to show his tribal affiliations, a huge lion's head across his chest. It was an intimidating stance that sent shivers down Ewan's back, as if the robber was proud to be a killer.

"Do you find defendant number three guilty or not guilty?

"Guilty." Now it was his turn to play to family and friends. Though as wide as he was tall, he made up for his shortness by jumping up and down, encouraged by shouts from the balcony. He started to punch the air and aimed a jabbing fist at the jury. The judge banged his gavel again demanding silence, with a further warning that he would clear the court if the noise continued. The guards from either end of the prisoners' bench stood menacingly in front of each robber and handcuffed them in turn behind their backs. They had just gone from defendants to prisoners, and the cuffs would curtail their antics. A further guard entered the dock, indicating playtime was over.

The judge turned to the prosecution bench and nodded. Prompted, Tom stood up and spoke clearly and strongly describing the effect the loss of their parents had on them both. It was simple and heart-wrenching. He called the attitude of the three men in the dock callous, heartless, and merciless, treating the court as a circus. "To kill our Labradors was a cold-hearted act no one could forgive. You and your families should be ashamed." As Tom sat, Ewan leant over and squeezed his shoulder. It was done.

Ewan watched the three convicted men standing now

with their heads bowed as the judge sentenced each to life, twenty-five years in prison. Ewan knew the description of the killings had a profound effect on Tom and Sarah, and the sentences would go a little way to giving them closure, but the massacre of the two Labradors hit them in its savagery, images they both would find extremely difficulty to wipe out. Ewan had looked away when the disturbing pictures of the killings were shown to the jury. There had not been a murmur then from the gallery. He doubted they could understand the gravity of the crimes perpetrated by their kith and kin. But the day was done, and escaping to Vineyard House would allow them to move on.

CHAPTER 51

"Ewan, please come and meet Graham," Sarah called from the kitchen. "He's with Tom, and they want your impartial opinion."

"I can maybe do ignorance; I'm not at ease with high finance."

"Just get in here; we need you." As Ewan entered the kitchen, Tom pointed to a fairly short, portly figure sitting on a counter stool. Ewan shook his hand and received a very strong, village pump welcome.

"Ewan, I'm Graham from the North, and don't believe all they say about me." Ewan detected a slight Geordie accent, which seemed out of keeping with the surroundings. He warmed to him straightaway.

"Okay, I'm Ewan from even further up North and very pleased to meet you." It was an encouraging start.

Tom asked him for an update on all his dad's affairs, and it was a lengthy list. Ewan was surprised at how many different strands tied Tom's dad to so many businesses, and they all seemed very successful. Graham said he had been in touch with the London office manned by a jack of all trades, who was previously a chambers' clerk, and a matronly-like secretary who had unbelievable contacts. The office acted as a go-between in the consultancy business and provided almost every service under the sun. Ewan could imagine entertaining of one sort or another might be on the list, but probably at the shadier end. On hearing these secrets, Ewan felt like an interloper in a family affair, yet Tom constantly asked for his thoughts and opinions. The sums of money mentioned were staggering and beyond Ewan's comprehension. The odd ten million rand seemed like small change in their discussions. When Yorkshire Yachts recent valuation of twenty million pounds was quoted by Graham, Tom nodded slowly and looked at Ewan with raised eyebrows. Ewan could only shake his head in bewilderment. The conversation turned to the disposal of assets, and it was evident Graham had done a brilliant job of bringing everything together. Ewan was amazed as each venture revealed either investment or interest in going concerns. Tom's dad was a very wealthy man, and Ewan felt uncomfortable hearing the detail. The others didn't seem to mind and were more concerned with the next steps.

Ewan sensed the tension rise when Graham raised the topic of Broadview House. Knowing that Sarah didn't want to be involved in anything to do with the house, which belonged to her by dint of the will, Tom suggested they all go for a walk along the vines and see the house from a distance. The vines were laden and looked ready to pick to Ewan's inexpert eye. In trying to lighten the mood, he asked Sarah for her professional opinion. "I know I'm an expert in wine because I have a knack with a bottle opener, but when will these grapes be ready to pick? And let me add that the use of screw-tops is one of the best advances in science. What do you think?"

"You Philistine. Don't you appreciate the care wine needs to be at its best. Look at these rows of heavily-laden vines. They didn't get here by accident. And in a few weeks, we'll turn them into nectar, and you talk about 'screw-tops'." The others started to laugh, with a crestfallen Ewan trying to hide his shame.

"That's right, Sarah, you tell him," was Tom's helpful riposte.

"Sorry, but Tom and I have been practising a great deal, and a cork only slows us down." Sarah kept up a running commentary on winemaking until they reached the top of a small hill and a break in the lines. Tom pointed to the outline of a house that now appeared quite close.

"Ewan, that is Broadview House. Dad wanted the Cape Dutch look with its grand ornately rounded gables from Amsterdam. He insisted on the white-washed walls and the thatched roofing because it's traditional, the same with the external wooden shutters. I don't know if you can make it out, but they are always in green and I've no idea why. Look, you can even see the blue shape of Table Mountain across False Bay. Dad liked the idea of being on the Constantia wine route. Where you see the dip in the coastline, that's Gordon's Bay, but nothing to do with gin, Sarah will tell you. It has a three-star Michelin rating and offers her speciality Chenin blanc to their discerning clients at whopping prices. Mind you, her chardonnay comes a close second, and we have become experts on the latter, haven't we, Ewan?"

Sarah interrupted to say she would like to go back, and Tom nodded. The court proceedings were still too raw for even a glimpse of the house.

CHAPTER 52

The approach to Broadview House was even more imposing than Esk Hall in Yorkshire. Everywhere was manicured to perfection. The lawns surrounded a snaking lake with a statue spouting water in the middle. As the car slowed on approaching the forecourt, the colonnaded portico showed the house meant business. The green outline of the shuttered windows was in stark contrast to the brilliant white of the building with the thatch adding a touch of grey. The twisting tall gables were imposing.

Ewan and Tom were in the back seat of the car with Graham in the front next to a very large, tough-looking driver. Ewan nudged Tom. "This sight is impressive. Does it feel like home? I can't imagine me being able to relax in a house this size."

"Not any more. Graham's already emptied the contents; they're in a warehouse now so we only have a shell here. All my memories are stored away as well. We just need to empty the safes then we're finished here, sad to say. Mum and Dad loved this place with its fantastic view of Table Mountain. It was a great backdrop for all their parties. Let's go inside. Graham has brought some bags for any paperwork, but I really don't know what to expect."

The guard and Graham stood at the front door, and Tom led Ewan to a back door off the kitchen, which opened into the garage. Tom pointed to a humidor fixed to the wall. "They're in there."

"What?"

"The cigar safe. By unlocking the front and swinging the contents to the side, hey presto, two safes. Dad was always suspicious of having safes in the house, and he thought not everyone liked cigars. Let's see if my unlocking skills will work. The combination is a mixture of our birthdays, so I should remember the numbers." The safe doors opened after some fumbling by Tom and a few swear words. "Ewan, if I hand things to you, can you stack them on the bench, please?" The relay started, and Ewan's eyes widened as very heavy gold bricks were passed to him. He couldn't believe their weight. The stack was getting bigger. "That seems all the heavy stuff, but here are some small soft bags Have a peek in them, but don't spill any." Ewan's eyes were on stalks as he opened a bag to find what he assumed to be diamonds: lots of them. Finally, Ewan could see the safe had given up all its contents. "That's it for this one, now the other."

"There's another?"

"Yup." The second safe was full of papers, and Ewan had difficulty stacking them neatly.

"What are these?"

"I think they're share certificates and title deeds. Just pile them up where you can. I'll get Graham to go through these before he gives them to the accountant or the lawyer. I'm sure they're all legit, but better be on the safe side. Right, that about does it. Let's bag this lot up. We can use that wheelie bin. It's a good disguise until we can off-load the contents into the car. Anybody watching will only think we're taking out the rubbish. Mind you, I've no idea how much the bricks and stones are worth. Graham has lined up assessors in the city, one for the diamonds and one for the bricks. We're going straight there. This will be what the robbers were after. I hope they bloody rot. It makes my blood boil. I still see their smug faces in the courtroom, pretending they were effing innocent. Let's get these piles bagged. I need to get out of here."

"Okay, but these bars are a trifle heavy. If we put them in those empty plant tubs and cover them up, we can get the strong-arm to come and move them."

"Good idea, but we can pocket the four small gem bags, though I hesitate to think what they're worth. There's a thriving Dutch gems trade in the city, and Graham has contacted a trustworthy dealer. I'll be glad when we can get this lot safely off our hands. You do know the driver is armed, don't you?"

"No, but now I feel a great deal better. Are we going straight to drop the stuff off?"

"Yes. We have two stops to make, and they're expecting us. The first is the diamonds and jewellery and the second, the bricks. All they are going to do is weigh and photograph what we have. Graham has instructed Peter to visit them later, which keeps us out of contact with the merchandise, so to speak. Let's get this all sorted."

Ewan wasn't sure the journey into the city, laden with potential loot, had been a sensible move, but he didn't say so. At every junction, the driver approached cautiously, with everyone's eyes out on stops. Ewan noticed the driver slowed down a hundred yards before any crossing or junction, then floored it. The theory was to reverse ambush anyone who thought of getting in the way. They left quite a few angry motorcyclists in their wake.

"Here is the first stop. That guy at the garage doorway has the registration of the car, and he'll let us in without stopping. Once inside, don't be surprised if there are guards with guns; it's normal here. The diamond trade has to protect itself. Give me the black bags, and I'll get out with the driver. We shouldn't be long: just time to get the stones and jewellery weighed and snapped." Ewan passed the bags over.

"Look, be bloody careful, and, at the first sign of trouble, get flat on the floor. I need you back here in one piece." After about ten minutes, Tom sauntered back nonchalantly to the car, as if he transported diamonds for a living. Back on the street, Ewan was as tense as ever. The bricks were next.

It was a similar procedure as they drew up in front of a nondescript building with a ramp that led up to massive iron gates, manned by very large men. This time the car was stopped, and the driver had a terse conversation with one of the guards. Sitting on the ramp made them vulnerable, and he said so in a loud voice. With photo IDs produced by all, they were waved into an inner courtyard, with more guards patrolling in front of another gate. As the barrier dropped behind them, the gates slowly opened, and they moved into what Ewan took to be an old unloading dock. A smiling face appeared at the steps, and Graham visibly relaxed when they recognised each other. A very large ape-like figure arrived carrying a video camera and started to film.

"Tom, is this normal?"

"It's just a precaution. They'll take all the bricks from the boot and film each one. We just sit tight here. Graham will get a receipt for the transfer, then we're done, and you can start relaxing."

"You bet. I feel like I'm in one of those heist movies. Are you sure we're not?"

"Look, you only played a bit part, and your Scottish accent won't have made it onto the soundtrack. Here's Graham. Let's get back to Vineyard House and some Chenin blanc".

CHAPTER 53

"Ewan, you seem to have gone quiet these last few days."

"It's been quite a whirlwind since I arrived here, and I feel a bit awkward with Sarah and Jerry. Don't get me wrong, they are splendid hosts, but I have difficulty relaxing as we're in their house, and we just can't be you and me."

"I know. But they really appreciated your being with them for the court appearance, and you say the right things when we eat or drink. They want you to be their roving ambassador for Chenin blanc; don't worry, I've told them that you have more experience with chardonnay and its after-effects. I'm storing all the missed opportunities; you wait until we get back – that's a promise."

"Right. I want to help, but Graham and Philip seem to have your interests well sewn up. I'm a bit lost here. Remember, you need to nail down Yorkshire Yachts before we leave, and there's lots to learn. Meeting the team and seeing the production line is the start of my learning curve. You probably know what goes on, so if I ask stupid questions, just give me the usual nudge."

"I definitely don't know it all, so ask away. It'll be a day of discovery for both of us. Our future."

CHAPTER 54

"Once we finish breakfast, we're off to Yorkshire Yachts, or YY as I now call it. That's my code in case anyone is listening in. Maybe I should change that to XX so it's not as obvious. I hope it lives up to the picture I've painted. I still love the area. It's spectacular, and the factory is located at the edge of Harbour Island breakwater in Gordon's Bay with the marina just in front. The shape of the bay is like a fishhook, which is what they used to call the place. Typically, an explorer turns up, and they have to call it after him, and, yes, he was Scots. It nestles at the foot of the Hottentot Mountains that go up to five thousand feet and overlook False Bay and Table Mountain. It's like a sandstone semi-circle, which gives the rosy glow and offers great natural protection from the storms created where the Atlantic and Indian oceans meet. There, brochure description over. Are you impressed? Does it sound exciting?"

"It does, but last night was just as exciting and good of Sarah and Jerry to give us space. I hope I appeared, and dare I say acted, more relaxed."

"Oh, you did that. Can't you see I'm still smiling? Let's only say you were more your old self. I know the visits to the repositories put you on edge, and you thought you were taking part in a heist á la film thriller. Let's just say that the baddies took a wrong turn at the crossroads where we almost totalled that bus. Don't get me wrong. Philip described the individual that has been making noises about a joint venture, and he hasn't understated the threat. Even the detective who ran the case briefed me on the current underworld pressures that are gang generated and drug related. We still need to think about how we avoid them. At least the valuables are now safe, and Graham said he'll get valuations by the end of the week. I expect the sums to be embarrassing. Give Dad his due: he was sharp when it came to investing and protecting his businesses. That's why I want YY to continue to be successful. Philip said there are sufficient liquid funds to do whatever we want, and that includes relocating to England."

"Sounds like all options are open. I agree the scenery is spectacular, but you've said the business atmosphere stinks. Have you mentioned anything about a possible relocation to the chap who runs the company?"

"No, not yet. We need to get a feeling for what's happening here. Once you've seen the place, I want us to sit down and talk it through before we even mention the subject. In the back of my mind, that property next to the sailing club in Southampton would make a brilliant location. I don't know how much they want for it, but there are ample liquid funds to purchase it and refurb. I know it will cost big bucks to transfer the whole lot, but if we get the timing right, we can minimise any disruption. What do you think?"

"I'm with you as ever, but this isn't a uni exercise. It's real, very real, with actual people. It'll be a major undertaking and picking the right people to manage it will be crucial. I've been impressed with Graham, and Peter sounds on the ball. How you broach the subject with the current management will be difficult. You said Niall, the CEO, is a New Zealander. He may want a change of location, or the challenge, or both."

"He's so easy-going, but sharp underneath. You're dead right. How to raise the subject is tricky. I'll emphasise the threats that've been made, and relocation possibilities in SA. Peter can come to the meeting and give the YY team a background brief with the odd hint about the security situation. What do you think?"

"Good idea, but we ought to discuss our misgivings with Peter before any meetings. We can give him a call and see what he thinks. I'm finding it hard to take in the dark side of what might be going on here."

"It's a revelation to me as well, but I'm really excited if we can pull it off. My tutor suggested a few headings to get me started, and he said a smart spreadsheet and timetable should involve good groundwork for the beginning of term. Adding the security angle might add spice for the term examiners. Now, if you're finished and have had enough of those pancakes, the car is ready whenever we are."

"It wasn't that many bloody pancakes; I just didn't want to upset the cook by leaving any. Let's go. Today should be a revelation and an education for me."

CHAPTER 55

Ewan felt Cape Town had a magnetic attraction for both of them. For Tom, it was almost a home from home; for Ewan, it was the splendour and scenery. The breakwater was an engineering marvel, stretching like a giant comma. Approaching the marina, they saw some pretty big yachts. A very neat parking area fronted an impressive building, and Ewan noticed the large lettering on the shed roofs. Yorkshire Yachts in brilliant red; you couldn't miss it. Standing in front of the imposing glass and metal company frontage was a tall youthful-looking male with an immaculately trimmed beard. Tom made the introductions.

"Niall, this is my partner, Ewan." We are dying to see your operation. My dad used to keep me up to date with your progress, and he always beamed when your name was mentioned. He enjoyed your continuous flow of new ideas, and the 3D printer was his main topic of conversation when yachts were mentioned. In fact, he could be quite a bore on the subject. Well, Ewan wants to learn all about it, as he can wind the subject into his thesis. He's doing fluid dynamics as his core subject. We'll both be starting our second year when we get back. Let's start the tour."

"Well you are both welcome. Let's go."

Ewan hung back most of the time as Tom was led through the labyrinth of corridors. The building was segregated into different halls with airlocks at each entrance. The giant 3D printer occupied one on its own. Ewan was suitably impressed. The machine was laying down another mould to start the next build. It was a brilliant practical demonstration with great photo opportunities. Ewan was introduced to Roy, the chief designer, and enjoyed talking about the design challenges. It seemed the toilet facilities on board were always the one area that needed maximum effort and tact to meet a client's aspirations. A gimballing toilet had addressed many a delicate discussion. The hands-on staff were keen to talk about what they did, and the know-how they had built up over time. Ewan absorbed what he could and packed the detail away believing it would make excellent fodder for the design part of his studies. In the hall next to the slipway, two yachts were in the final process, and they looked resplendent and very expensive. Ewan took some photos to send to Fred, including close-ups of the 3 D printer, a new subject to feed Fred's appetite for research.

Finally, Niall said lunch was calling. They entered through two sets of doors and the smell of curing plastic gradually disappeared and was replaced by that of highly polished wood and leather. The complete change in surroundings caught Ewan by surprise.

The so-called "client facility" was a mock-up of the internal cabin of the current model, arranged to make a buyer feel at home with luxury. Everything sparkled or shone, and it made a superb boardroom. Lunch was laid out with the food following nautical themes of waves and sails, a truly impressive design experience for the humble sandwich. Ewan's jaw dropped, and Tom had to nudge him to close it. "Just take this in your stride," he whispered. "Potential clients have money and need familiar moneyed surroundings. Niall said this is good practice. Let's tuck in."

Back at Vineyard House at dinner, Ewan and Tom recounted their day's visit with an upbeat assessment to put Sarah at ease. Tomorrow's boardroom meeting would prove a challenge to keep discussions positive.

CHAPTER 56

They both agreed today would be a crucial meeting with Niall. Tom would start the conversation by raising the possibility of opening a second facility at Southampton to mirror Harbour Island. Ewan would then outline the warehouse for sale next to the "stuck-up" sailing club. The idea was to get Niall on board to design the new facility, and, at the same time, get a feel for how he saw the security situation developing. No mention was to be made of transferring the whole operation to the UK.

There was a welcoming smell of coffee as they entered the boardroom. The table resembled the hull of a boat topped with the ever-present walnut planking, a magnificent statement. They all helped themselves to coffee, then sat around the prow of the model, almost alongside each other, confrontation free.

"Niall, thanks for yesterday's excellent guided tour. We were both impressed with such a friendly welcome and the bountiful spread you laid on. Ewan can't grasp your take on the humble sandwich, is that right, Ewan?"

"Absolutely. I will be on a mission when we get back to uni to raise the sandwich profiles, though I'm not sure the all-chilli sandwich will get my vote. It almost blew my head off; you might have noticed."

"My pleasure, and you'd be surprised how many of our guests remark about their fondness for chilli, but I admit it's an acquired taste that probably has still to reach Scotland. Right, Tom, fire away with your questions."

"What we saw was very impressive. Your expertise has been hard earned and my dad was astonished at the way the facility evolved, especially with the introduction of the 3D printer. Ewan's done some property searches, and we may have a possible solution for a sister facility to concentrate on the launch of the Yorkshire 55 class. Over to you, Ewan."

"Niall, I'm not an expert, so I may ask some very basic questions to find out what you would need or like to see if a similar plant could be just as successful. The property we have seen has a warehouse that sits next to a ramped jetty in an inner Southampton harbour. Way back, it was a sea-plane base. The warehouse is approximately fifty thousand square feet, not sure what that is in metres, but it's in reasonable condition says the advert, so no major demolition would be needed, and there is ample space for expansion. You would have a blank canvas, except that the slipway is a listed structure and has to be preserved, but it should be a valuable addition. The footprint for any construction needs to stay in the current boundaries. What would it take to design a factory to cope with the demands of carbon fibre, 3D printing, and end-to-end production? Conveniently, there's ample berth space and easy access to Southampton Waters from a substantial concrete dock. Tom said you would be the man to consult and maybe do the build."

"That's a fast one. It would certainly be a great challenge, and we have our current production system moving towards full automation. Introducing new methodology here is no easy task. Starting from new would be bliss." Tom gave a sympathetic nod.

"Is it something you would be interested in doing for us?" Tom asked quietly. "Obviously, it would need to be made worth your while, and there might be some commuting to the UK."

"You know, the UK is a place I've always wanted to visit. That was where I was bound when I stopped off here for a bit of a rest, and that was eight years ago. Your dad was too good an employer to miss the chance of doing my own thing, and helping his dream come true was enough reward. He was generous to a fault, despite his bluff exterior. I felt I got to know him. Maybe I can make yours come true as well."

"Niall, it would be brilliant to get you on board. Let's talk later in the week. Philip, dad's lawyer, has already given us some headings to consider, so we could all sit down and sketch out the way ahead. Don't laugh, but I'm using this possible new business idea to double as my second-year term paper. Your inputs would help me avoid naïve bloomers. We'll give you a call to arrange another get-together. We're keeping the subject close to our chests at the moment. And Ewan has been promised a teach-in by Roy, your brilliant designer, who has even found some of his original hull and profile sketches; they can speak fluid dynamics at our next visit. And thanks again for the amazing spread. Ewan, our chief sandwich maker, may have a few questions as to some of the fillings later. We can then ask our uni canteen to be creative. Cheese and pickle are definitely passé."

On the drive back, Tom was elated. "That was good value. I like the way Niall is always open and positive. We didn't spill the beans on a complete withdrawal, and the overture to Niall could start the sequence. You'll agree that broaching the possible full relocation will need very careful and tactful handling, but in our exchanges when we refer to the business plan, we ought to devise a reason for any activity that could give our ultimate plan away. Any thoughts on creating some sort of smokescreen?"

"We could always indicate that we're preparing for a competition or race. You've experience of that. As to Niall's response, he came across as genuine, and he can certainly lay on a spread. And, yes, I enjoyed the sandwiches, but responding after a mouthful of chili was impossible. I must have drunk a gallon of tonic water. That action may backfire on me soon. But I'm keen to talk to Roy again, and pump him for the secrets behind his design. I'll send the detail to Fred to see if he thinks it would help the flying boat project. I know he loves to follow up on the detail

CHAPTER 57

Sarah had arranged Xmas events to include only a few close friends; the atmosphere was low-key by mutual consent. Normally, their parents would have thrown large parties with tons of guests. This holiday season could never be the same. Ewan and Tom had enjoyed visiting the factory and made themselves very busy the week prior to the holiday; their learning curves exceeding expectations.

"Tom, you know that my sessions with Roy are incredible and match what I have to study in year two. If I stayed here an extra week with you and drained Roy of boat info, it would be a better way of starting term. He's tied in the theory with the practice. I even have a memory stick with his initial design approach and all the calculations and reasoning, which I know Fred will devour. I'll send a summary of what I can learn here to my tutor and ask for a week's starting delay. It would mean me going back with you on the tenth, and we can hold hands, metaphorically in public. Does that make sense? It looks like you'll run out of time here."

"Definitely. I'd love that. Philip's marshalling all the paperwork for signature before I go to get the will executed. There is a mountain to get through. It seems Dad's funds are spread widely, including Switzerland. God knows what the total will be, but we'll need some smart and reliable individual to guide us. Norm, Dad's UK accountant, will be a crucial contact. Moving money and paying people is his domain, and he knows the bank account inside out. Dad's UK liaison office, which Graham will oversee, will be a good source of legwork to get us started, despite there being only two of them."

"Shit, Tom. This is way over my head. Does Philip have a reliable legal contact in the UK that you can use who knows the score? With the amounts that seem to be growing by each revelation, you're sitting on a huge pile, and that always brings grief with it. On the other hand, I, with no money, have problems of a different sort, but they're manageable, provided you're kind to me, which, of course, you are. That puts it all into perspective. I like where I am."

"So, do I, and we need to relax more. Niall has invited us to the company BBQ this afternoon at Bikini Beach, which is just next door to the factory. It's a beautiful setting, and we'll be able to meet most of their team. We can both wear our Bermuda shorts, and, of course, my pair are quite special."

"You can say that again. It does your profile wonders. And it's New Year's Eve, and I've always had to wear the thickest pullovers ever, with socks to match, to beat the challenging Scottish weather. I had better take some photos of my shorts to tease them back home." They left in a rundown jeep for the beach in good spirits.

"Tom, this is a bit of a let-down. Where's the Bentley?"

"It isn't good to advertise your wealth here. Niall says

that there are gangs that see the expensive cars as easy pickings, even when there is muscle in the front. So, we take precautions. Nothing to get worried about." So, Ewan promptly worried. The heist scenario was too fresh in his mind.

Niall welcomed them warmly and made introductions to almost everyone. It was hard to talk with the music blaring out. Most people were shouting, and that was how Ewan was introduced to their chief operations officer by the name of Karl Weisbaden. He was a larger-than-life character, overweight, and sporting a mass of facial hair. The moustache fused into a ginormous beard, and he had the timely look of Father Christmas. His accent revealed his Germanic origins, and Ewan warmed to him. Tom was recounting part of his homebound trip and the yacht's handling when there was a commotion at the edge of the group. Two of the company's minders were confronting a group of youths who were trying to enter the roped-off area declaring that the beach was theirs from birth. Philip, who was standing nearby, started taking photos of the group, which seemed to send them even higher up the angry scale. Two more minders appeared, and a police car cruised to a halt on the nearby promenade. As the officers got out, the group started to back off to the other side of the dunes, and all seemed defused.

"Tom, that could have turned nasty," declared Ewan. "They looked like they meant business."

"Yup, but the minders are used to the locals creating trouble. Philip will pass copies of the photos to the police. It always helps to identify them for future reference. Some of the staff here will also probably know their faces. Here's

Philip. What was that all about?"

"We don't as yet know who they are, but we guess they were encouraged to create a scene by the associates of the gang who went to prison. We've had it before. They rob to fund their main business, drugs. It's a growing menace here. The police will match their faces to previous incidents to build a picture. You remember, I said in my very first phone call to you that a problem may be developing. Well, we've had a few of these, together with threats to some of the staff, so we have to try and stay ahead of them. Niall has increased security with a complete suite of cameras operating 24/7. In the week before the court case, the guards managed to stop an arson attack before they could gain access. It's something we have to live with, but the money spent on security is good insurance. And we are not the only ones in the area having to bolster security. Drug running via other yachting enterprises was revealed during a recent trial. The local gangs use every means to get the drugs out of Cape Town and into the regions for distribution to the surrounding hotspots where sun and sex fuel the demand. Here's Niall."

"Sorry, guys. They've gone. The police recognise them so will pay them a visit to try and resolve any issues. But with one dead and the rest of the gang of three in jail, they may not take too kindly to being warned off, and the family of the one who was shot have vowed to get their own back on the police. They're part of a large clan based in the northern townships. I don't see an early resolution to the problem. We just have to get on with the business. Speaking of which, we are taking our latest issue out on the water for its sea trials tomorrow; do you want to join us? Tom, we can use your recent experience to see if we can make the boat more user-friendly."

"You bet. Ewan and I would love to, wouldn't you, Ewan?" Ewan gave a thumbs-up. Tom nodded. "Ewan needs the experience, and he'll find out how fluid the water can be when it's bent round a perfectly shaped hull."

"As long as I don't get in the way. And I only have one set of sailing rig, so I better not get wet." They all sucked their breath in with fake sympathy.

CHAPTER 58

Clearing Island Harbour breakwater under power into False Bay, the yacht started to feel the swell. This was the only sea trials the craft would go through before it departed for Dubai and its well-heeled owner. Tom was in his element and appeared everywhere on the yacht at the same time. Ewan, with no evident purpose, was trying to make himself scarce, while the crew proved that the binnacles and winding mechanisms did what they were supposed to do. He had only one pair of deck shoes, and, if they got wet, he would have to survive on-board in his cotton socks. Everywhere was covered in polythene or foam packing. The reveal would be for the client only. There was to be no toilet usage, so peeing over the side was the order of the day. With the kitchen out of bounds, a hamper of sandwiches filled the breach. They were posh ones with oodles of cress, accompanied by strange and, to Ewan's uneducated eye, exotic nibbles. He made surreptitious tests to check for hidden chillies.

Table Mountain acted as guardian with the yacht going through its paces. Niall indicated that they would normally stay in the bay, but, for Ewan, they were going to turn Cape Point and reach the Cape of Good Hope where the two big oceans meet. He could then say he had sailed in the Atlantic and Indian Oceans on the same day. It was a heady moment with everyone grinning, Ewan included. He couldn't believe how much the others deferred to Tom, and not because he owned them. He was meticulous with his actions and comments. They listened while he explained which parts of the fixings and structures got in his way or were a pain to operate. On the other hand, Ewan became the chief sandwich operator. In such brilliant and unique surroundings, he found it difficult to relate to his previous life.

The return to dock was a bit of a show-off with the yacht passing quite a few marinas, and a big shipyard. There was a surprising toot from what looked like a roll-on/roll-off – "RoRo" – ferry. Niall said the ferry was nearing completion and would be bound for St Nazaire in France to get its innards sorted, then to the Channel Islands to replace an old one that was going to the knacker's yard. Ewan decided there was more going on at sea than people realised. Tom and Ewan exchanged many nods and headshakes as each revelation surfaced.

While the yacht was being put to bed, Niall, Tom, and Ewan sat on a bench in the car park. "Thanks, Niall, for a brilliant day, and I think Ewan enjoyed it as well. The yacht looked good and just slid through the water. I thought the automatic keel boards help take the sting out of the water. Ewan can wax eloquent when he's next in class."

"My pleasure. Roy appreciated your ideas on the little things that get in the way. He'd like to sit down with you and see how we can improve on the mechanics when under power and sail. Now, there is something I'd like to raise just between us. You mentioned replicating the business in Southampton, and it would make good economic sense. But, and I shouldn't say this, the nigger in the woodpile is exactly that. I'm getting vibes that make me uneasy, and I've not said this to anyone else. Till now, we have always paid over the odds, and it has, dare I say it, bought a certain degree of loyalty. The atmosphere is changing. The mafia tentacles reached here from Italy decades ago, and the clans and drug lords are filling the current political void with corruption. You can buy anyone in office. I have a feeling that some of the new staff came onboard for different reasons, despite our caution. A couple have turned out to be firebrands, and it's impossible to get rid of them. I hope I'm not speaking out of turn, and I don't want to embarrass you, but a few of us have been mulling over the idea of relocating to avoid what we see as the inevitable change taking place in business here. Politics and graft are taking over. The clan heads are so into drug-running that makes any clean business a target for them. Cape Yachts, the smart marina we passed, were raided by the police and the drugs haul went into millions."

"Well, Ewan and I are strangers to whatever is changing here, and your advice would be much appreciated." Tom and Ewan exchanged knowing glances. "Where would you locate to?"

"I think that until the President either gets kicked out or imprisoned, all of SA will become a problem, and, for people like us, families will become vulnerable. Sad to say but anywhere in Europe looks a better bet. For most operators, business stability in build and supply are paramount. I know that a willing and capable workforce is needed, but we can recruit from anywhere provided we have the basic management and skills in place. All our computery is in the cloud and well protected. Most of our specialist suppliers are in either France or Germany, which only leaves the 3D printer and stock at risk. Shipping them wouldn't be a problem."

"When Ewan and I mentioned the possible option of setting up a similar base in Southampton, did that ring any bells?"

"It sure did. I've done some legwork in terms of space needed, new staff numbers, and shipping tasks. Do you want me to elaborate?"

"Absolutely. It would be a huge undertaking, but the site we saw could make perfect sense if we can secure it. The initial purchase price and remodelling wouldn't pose any financial problems, but there might be timescale issues."

"Okay, I suggest we meet with my top team, and run through the problems and our solutions. Remember, we are talking about a New Zealander, a German, an Aussie, and a Dutchman, so the answers should be international. Moving lock, stock, and barrel would need careful and accurate planning to avoid disappointing any potential clients and keep out of the reach of the clans. Once we agree a plan, it's just a matter of timing."

"That makes complete sense. We go back to the UK in a week's time. Having an outline plan by then would be excellent. I'd want Philip, our lawyer, and Graham who holds the fort at this end, to be involved. We'll need to keep the discussions close to our chest. It may be safer to meet at Vineyard House rather than here. We don't want word to get out. From the outset, I want to say that any relocation of people would be generously rewarded, both in terms of salary and upheaval expenses. We have a subsidiary company in the UK that can make initial enquiries about the land for sale. That would be a top priority. Again, we don't have any financial worries in that direction, even if we have to pay a premium. I'll give you a ring to set up a suitable time. Anyway, thanks for a revealing day."

"And I can second that. Serving sandwiches at sea has always been an ambition of mine." Ewan waved his hands towards heaven.

CHAPTER 59

Back in their room, they flopped on the bed holding hands. "That yacht outing was one of the most enjoyable times I've spent on the water," Tom said with emphasis. "It was hectic and serious at the same time. I think Niall and Roy appreciated my input, but perhaps the Dubai sheik won't be pulling on the sheets as I did, while desperate for a pee. He'll have staff for that. The sheik's brother has completed on the other one we saw. They pay eye-watering sums for these boats. I know it pays all the wages and overheads and brings in a healthy profit, but it feels obscene to be attached to this money-making machine. And Niall really surprised me with that suggestion, which means we don't have to broach what we had in mind. It looks like he wants to move the whole operation. The criminal pressures were new to me. I suppose we're a bit naïve. God knows what these clans are up to. We need to escape intact."

"That also caught me by surprise and is fantastic news for us. We'll need to list as many questions as we can think of. From my lowly status as a bottom-scraper, using your dad's funds to survive the business is admirable. He'd be proud. When I had the chance to talk to Niall, I gained the impression that there was more going on behind the scenes than he wanted to let on. I mentioned the beach altercation, and he just grimaced. Talking to him in private will give us a better feel for what we would be up against. And by the way, who and where is this UK office?"

"It's the flat, or more specifically, the spare room. We only need one bed, don't we?" Philip has suggested that I set up a holding company to umbrella all Dad's assets, shares, and funds. He's told me that Dad has an accountant in the UK; he's Norm, an Essex boy and sharp as a tack as regards the Revenue. We'll meet him when we get back. Philip says he's a rock that'll provide protection on all avenues, and that might include his contacts who know about the shadier elements that could affect the business. We need to think of what we do with YY if and when we leave. That part of it scares me. Remember, we also have the use of the UK consultancy office. Dad called it York Central, and the woman of indeterminate age who ran it was called Mo. She knew everyone in the business and beyond. Her contact book was to die for. She solved problems before people knew they had them. She'll be a fantastic asset."

CHAPTER 60

Sarah had agreed to host the meeting at Vineyard House. Ewan and Tom sat at the kitchen table outlining the proposal that Niall had made. She was all for it and offered a few headings of her own. She hinted that she and Jerry had already discussed moving to the UK to be safe and manage the vineyard at arm's length. Tom looked at Ewan when she suggested it, but Ewan could see Sarah's shoulders drop with a certain air of resignation. She said the incident at the beach BBQ was a sign of things to come, and nothing in the world was going to jeopardise their baby. Ewan sensed that she and Tom were of a like mind, and that change was in the air, and not just in this household or business.

Sarah's lunch spread was magnificent, as was the Chenin blanc. Tom led the discussions, with Niall and Philip adding their opinions. George seemed to wait his turn until discussions turned to the threat. He, too, had bad vibes about the black power shifts, and gave a rundown of the past six months in the Cape area with a disturbing conclusion on the drug clans whose hold was throttling the past freedoms with political activists demanding recompense for past sins against them. His conclusion was that there was too much simmering below the surface, and with the President's court case looming, the distraction was enough for the mafia to start spreading its tentacles. Moving the operation to the UK would be tricky once the plan surfaced, so sleight of hand and subterfuge were his watchwords. Ewan had been quiet for a while, feeling the talk was above him, but he decided to wade in.

"Speaking from the outside looking in, why don't we just get that RoRo ferry to park at the company jetty, and load everything on. If we helped pay for the transit to St Nazaire, with an added contribution for going via Southampton, we could escape the growing problem here, and establish the company in an ideal spot in yacht-selling land. I know we would have to get a move on with purchasing the plot, but we probably don't need to do 'new build'; from what I could see, the building and parking areas are currently used for car storage and are clean and dry."

"Ewan, a light-bulb moment. I like the idea of keeping everything simple, and that RoRo has plenty of room. What do you think, Niall?"

"Pardon the expression, but let's see if the idea floats. I'll make soundings, but we need to keep this under wraps until we have a decent plan. I can't afford the workforce to down tools while we still have the two boats to prep for Dubai, and there are security issues to keep them drug-clean, hence the constant surveillance cameras. Tom, you have another week here; can you get a steer on whether getting the property is possible and in what timescale? You may need to pay over the odds to get a quick secure."

"Well, Dad had a small company offshoot in London we call York Central, just two people, the director and his Miss Moneypenny, though we all called her Mo. They were adept at getting anything done through a raft of companies. They're now on Graham's payroll, but I've kept a golden share in the consultancy, so we can get them to set the ball rolling. Finance isn't a problem; it's just the mechanics that take time. From the photos that a friend of ours, Fred, has sent, and we don't know how recent they are, the offices adjacent to the warehouse look solid enough, though I've no idea if there is any asbestos to contend with, but money should remove any roadblocks. What do you think, Philip?"

"You've put me on the spot, but the problem you'll face here – we all face here – is the destabilising influence of the continuous feed of bad news. Ewan's suggestion of preparing for a race is oblique enough to make total sense to anyone listening in. Once the goods are on the high seas, they would be untouchable, but I don't know what timescale you can target in the Southampton build, though surprise is in your favour. You do hold some valuable cards, Tom. Niall can draw up the spec and send you a video of the current set-up to help planning. I'm happy, at your expense of course," he said smiling, "to visit the UK, and my brother works there, and can draw up the necessary paperwork. I'm sure Niall would welcome the opportunity to visit the UK and plot what facilities he would need. It would make a good start." A phone went off and they all looked at one another. It was Niall's. He popped out of the room.

While they were discussing the possible bail-out to the UK, Niall came back into the room. All eyes turned in his direction. His face was sombre and dark. He spread his arms wide. "I've just taken a call from Karl's wife. He's been robbed at knife point. They got his cheap Rolex copy, but he lost quite a bit of blood from the arm injury, so they've taken him to hospital. I'm going to scoot off there straightaway. I'll put my mind to our discussions and talk to you tomorrow."

They sat around the table as if at the last supper. Each waiting for the other to make some reassuring remarks, but there were none available. Tom felt he was responsible for all the staff, but he could see Sarah was agitated. "This country is going down the drain fast. These people, left to their own devices, are happy for anarchy to reign. They think it balances all the harm done to them from Day One, but they seem to forget they have been in power for twenty years, and done sod-all, and they're all high on drugs. I think we should leave them to it. The vineyard is better managed at arm's length, accepting a standard loss to the clans, and receive a profit based on their take. The wine should still be the same. Then, when the mafioso get their comeuppance as they inevitably will, we can all return. Rant finished," Sarah said forcefully. Tom glowed and smiled at Sarah.

"Right, and I would like to second my sister, something I never dared do when we were fighting kids, and agree we desperately need to acknowledge the reality of what is happening here. I'll start the ball rolling if you, Philip, would get a date in your diary to come to the UK. George, can we meet on the Thursday before we leave to draw up an action list with timescales? You'd better brief Mo on the change of circumstances, and I'll ask her to make the initial offer on the premises. We can use YY as the code name for the project. Ewan and I will set up an office in the Southampton flat to manage all our correspondence, rather than the consultancy, until we can establish a better base, which I hope will be alongside our snooty sailing club neighbours. I don't want to jump the gun, but we will be selling tickets when we block the access to their car park. This is going to be an exciting ride." Tom looked at everyone and Ewan was grinning the most.

CHAPTER 61

The luggage was stacked up in the hall of Vineyard House. The driver and minder were ready. When Tom took baby Max into his arms, Ewan was touched by the noises Tom made. The moment of sadness registered, and the cloud took some time to disperse. Tom looked towards Ewan and noticed the shadow. "What's the matter?"

"Nothing. We need to get a move on."

"Don't you want to hold Max?"

"Tom, I do," Ewan whispered, "and he's absolutely gorgeous. But it's something I can never give you. That's reality. That's me."

"Shit. I'm sorry. I didn't mean to ..."

The farewells were sad, muted, and genuine. Ewan hugged Sarah, and she again whispered that godsends don't come often. Jerry joined the hug, and Ewan felt wanted.

As the car left the sanctuary of the vineyard and with the driver and strong-arm aboard, Tom grabbed Ewan's hand and whispered, "Look, you are my world now. I don't want it any other way. Family is family, but you are it. If we want children, we'll make them, just you and I." Their eyes met, held, and a flood of relief swamped Ewan.

"Sorry if I gave the wrong impression. It's just that I

can only give you all that I have, and there are times that that may not be enough, and it frightens me."

"I want you and need you as you are. Forget all this business crap. We have both been through enough shit to recognise that we need to make our own happiness. You make me bloody happy. I just want to do the same for you."

"You do. It's when we are on our own that I feel free. It's difficult to work out what I should say when we meet people, and I'm out of my depth."

"You don't realise that the things you say or whisper to me are the perfect words to trigger how I should respond. Please don't stop doing that. It gives me a warm feeling that we are in this together. And, when you think of it, we are the same in bed."

"Just wait till we get back to the flat, and I'll remind you what you said."

CHAPTER 62

The flat hadn't moved. Everything was the same, except for the subtle scent of wild rhubarb. Claire and Chris had lunch on the table and chilled bottles of wine in decorative coolers. They hugged one another and conversations rode over each other. "Let's decide that we can have one minute to recall the last month then shut up." The room was filled to bursting with too many smiles. "Ewan, you go first."

"Must I? Oh, well, here goes. I went with Tom to SA. It wasn't exactly a good time of year for both of us, but we got through it. Tom can now put the bad part behind him. We had a quiet Hogmanay, almost. I've met a great boat designer who's helping me to understand fluid dynamics, and I even did some practical by sailing round the Cape. I am now an aficionado on Chenin blanc, and training for my Master of Wine. That's it."

"I should have said 'ladies first'. Sorry, Claire."

"Okay. I'll spare Eric's blushes and let you both know that we had a marvellous Christmas, together. And I mean together. I've even met his family. We've been sailing in a Halcyon Twenty-seven, and made it to Cherbourg and back, together. We now have no secrets. Bet that surprises you. Anyway, the time, dare I say it, has just sailed by.

Hopefully, more to follow. Now it's Eric's turn. Watch what you say."

"As you can tell, I'm currently under the spell of a woman. She was skipper on the way over the Channel, and she can be right bossy. I was skipper on the way back, and I can tell you, she doesn't like taking orders. But, with us both wet and weary, it seems we can get along. Meeting my parents was quite a challenge, but they took to her. I couldn't get a word in edgewise."

"That's not true."

"See, you're at it again. Anyway, New Year was spent walking along the beach and acting as if we had only just met, but in a different context, if you know what I mean. The flat was a brilliant bolthole, and we even entertained Claire's sister and boyfriend. We were just practising domestic bliss, but the wine helped. There's still plenty left, I think. But welcome back. It's good to see you both again."

"Well, Ewan will tell you it was a difficult time for me and my sister Sarah. I'll be honest; the court case, and even the preliminaries, were a nightmare. That, together with sorting out my parents' affairs, left us frustrated and tired. We stayed with my sister at her house among the vineyards. It was a great oasis of calm. Ewan has kept my spirits up, despite us both battling memories. There was so much to cover, and the yacht building company may need a new home. You probably don't know, but things are pretty bad security-wise. There are clans operating outside the law. Robberies and drug-dealing are rife. Rampant bribery and corruption have taken over. Transferring the operation to here is probably our only option. There are derelict premises near the snooty sailing club that may be available to re-house the yacht company. It'll take lots of planning, interlaced with oodles of common sense. We would like your support. And you may have guessed that Ewan and I are an item. You might have seen that coming. The rings are for real. We can toast to that. It doesn't matter if it's in chardonnay or Chenin blanc."

CHAPTER 63

The first day back in Uni for both of them was hectic. They had to go their separate ways. It felt strange after all the recent togetherness. Their timetables clashed, so it was evening back at the flat before they could compare notes.

"Right, Ewan, how was it for you? Do you know if you're now behind in the learning game?"

"Funnily, no. It seems the week we were away, the so-called lectures just ended up with tales of the holidays and individual chats with the tutor, and I had mine today. When I spouted what we had done and especially my teach-in with Roy, he was impressed. The idea of using a 3D machine to build a scale model replicating the hull research had him stunned. He even suggested that funds might be available for materials. He wanted more detail, so I've already asked Fred for any drawings and spreadsheets that we can build on and sent him Niall's YY video and Roy's design paperwork. I emailed Fred's mum asking if we were overloading Fred, and she replied that it's one of the best things that has happened to him. He shows quite a bit of unexpected spark when he gets the emails. It makes me feel better after deserting him.

My tutor thought that taking our group idea forward

would make good subject matter, and at the same time register the requisite headings for the spring term. I did tell him that the timescale for hard experiment is uncertain, but he said the paperwork and research was more important than playing with toys. I said you can't hide crap from a 3D printer – the proof was in the cooking. He said he didn't mean to imply that the result would be wasted, but I just said politely, 'Watch this space.' And that must be the first time I have ever 'kicked against the pricks'. I was quite fired up, and I enjoyed the experience. Is this my coming of age?"

"Is that a sexual question to your partner, or a theological argument to your tutor? I prefer you as you are. I know I've said it before, but you bring me so much warmth and peace. You ask the questions I'm just beginning to think about. I don't want you to change; I don't want us to change. You're my rock. For me, what you say goes."

"Look Tom, I feel bloody comfortable in your company. I don't think we've had a proper argument yet. I would hate business to change that."

"It won't. You've probably got more nous than me. I'm a good listener. It should be fun sorting out YY. What do you think?"

"I get the feeling that money isn't going to be a problem, so what we do is down to you and me. Provided we get best advice, I agree with the 'fun' idea. But we have to be serious when dealing with anyone who might try and take advantage of our youthful appearance. None of them know we have both seen the darker side of life, and its maturing effect. I trust Niall and his senior staff that we met, and you have Philip and Graham to protect your back. Philip had good things to say about Norm, the accountant from

Essex, so your dad picked well. I was thinking that, as well as ourselves, we could include Claire and Eric in a holding company. Between us, we should be able to cover most business aspects."

"I'm all ears."

"Right. We can call it something like Seahorses Limited and all be directors. You can be in charge of strategy and policy, I can do operations, Eric can do technical, and Claire can do the cooking. Sorry, only joking. Don't ever tell her I said that; she'd kill me. She would be good for finance and admin. I'm just thinking aloud, but if Seahorses bought the land and refurbed the premises, it could then rent to a newly located YY. If anything happened to YY, the company asset would be protected. We could either operate salaries or a share scheme, not that the figures would be big. We would all be part-time while we learned our trades. As to finding dosh to start it all up, you would need to decide which pot it might come from. Did you call the estate agents about the site?"

"Look, I like the idea and agree entirely with what you've said. And I did call Ratt & Pearson. Eventually, they put me on to some precious individual who asked what company or agent I was calling on behalf of. I said that all I wanted was the site's price to make an informed decision for my principal. I finally got out of him that it's offers over three and a half million. He told me the land is owned by the local council, and there are numerous riders attached. He gave me a number to arrange viewing. I said my Principal would be in the area next week. He mumbled that it was short notice, so I said what notice would he like and would A3 size be suitable, but it was lost on him. I was beginning to seethe."

"Why don't the four of us turn up on our bikes just to see the look on his face as Claire takes charge?"

"Sounds perfect. We can ask Claire to be 'ballsy' when she talks to him. Being involved in a company with all the trimmings would help Claire and me gain kudos towards our Business Administration credits. We all get on, and something practical like this ties in with you and Eric as well. With our four brains, we should be able to outsmart any opposition. Let's have a meeting with them to see what they think. I expect people we meet may not take us too seriously at first, but I relish the challenge. What about you?"

"As long as our studies don't get in the way, I'm all for it. We'll probably have to be quite regimented in the time we spend and how we spend it. Your course work should help, even when we step out of the curriculum from time to time. If and when Niall accepts the challenge, his shoulders will take the majority of the burden. Claire can be quite feisty, and that won't do us any harm when we're dealing with estate agents, surveyors, architects and the like. When Philip comes, I'm sure she'll enjoy his approach, and it'll give her ammo for her coursework. It should work and keep us in the exciting bracket of life. We have both had enough knocks to decide it's pay-back time."

CHAPTER 64

"Ewan, you finished in there? I need a pee."

"Just about. Cross your legs."

"That's not funny. How come you take so long?"

"Come in. I'm just finishing my moustache shape."

"But you haven't got any hair on your lip."

"Yes, but I'm just preparing the ground. We need to have a tash-growing competition to make us look more mature and business-like. It'll help to build up image gravitas in our new company roles. People will then give us respect."

"They will take us seriously enough when they see the colour of your money. Wow, I needed that."

"Now wash your hands like a good boy."

"Shut up and finish in here. They'll be here in half an hour, and you need to smarten up. And don't forget, Niall will be here in over a week's time, so there's lots to discuss before then."

The knock on the door signalled the arrival of Claire and Eric. As usual they were spot on with timing. It was three o'clock on a bright January day. "Make yourselves at home. Tom is tarting himself up in the loo, and that might take some time. I'll put the kettle on; it's a trifle too early for anything stronger. We've loaded some of our pics from SA on my laptop. Please browse and pretend not to get bored."

"Ah, Tom. Is that Jo Malone or Old Spice?" Ewan queried.

"Hi, all. It happens to be Nautica, which I thought appropriate. Claire will give a detached opinion during the welcoming hug."

"Tom, you smell wonderful as ever. Eric will eventually run out of Brut, and I look forward to you giving him your leftovers."

"I don't need leftovers. I'm just waiting for them to bring back Lifebuoy soap that my dad swore by. Right, Tom, what is this special meeting you mentioned?"

"Okay. Niall, the YY CEO, is arriving in ten days' time from SA to see a possible location for the company. There have been further incidents of drug smuggling around Table Bay needing a large police presence. Everywhere is tense, and the lid may blow off soon, hence the urgency. We're putting him up in the Travelodge next to the Uni. He won't be here for long. I know I've mentioned the plot of land that would make a good base if YY moves here. I found out the price, and finance isn't a problem, but managing the project might be. So, we thought it would be great to co-opt yourself and Claire and the four of us form a company to manage the buy and refurbishment. We have plenty of funding; my Dad was canny with his money, and we can use it to further his idea of a Yorkshire class yacht. At the same time, we can use the expertise of YY to develop the floatplane idea using their know-how and, crucially, the 3D printer. Fred has already sent me his latest calculations, and he has done his research on electric powered aeroplanes, but it's all beyond me. We even have to stop using the word 'engines' and start saying 'drivetrains'. Something to do with battery power that doesn't use an engine.

Anyway, as to the business side, we would all be on expenses, with some share options that Dad's accountant will propose. What we do mustn't interfere with our uni programme, but I think we can all use the project as a vehicle for our second term's work. What about it? Claire?"

"Sounds just up my street. When do we begin? Sorry, I don't yet speak for Eric."

"I am Eric and one half of the external team. But what she says goes. I think it'll be good for our morale, and the uni project will get a boost from experts."

"Brilliant. Thanks. Let's skip the tea and break out a bottle to celebrate. I'll let Ewan decide whether it should be chardonnay or Chenin blanc. We've already done some delving. The niceties of setting up a company will be done by one of Dad's consultancy companies, and I can expect control of the bank accounts next week. Norm, the accountant, will set us up with an accounts programme. Claire, I think you used Xero as an accounts package in your first year; we could use that."

"We did, but it was like monopoly money. As long as everything tallied in the end, it didn't matter. This will be real money off a real tree. All the zeros need to be in the right place. Mind you, Eric always keeps an eye on me."

"Well, I do that automatically; it's called fatal attraction."

"I'm flattered, but we'll have to put it on an official footing - the arithmetic, I mean, and stop laughing. Tom, it's your money. I better get to know your accountant intimately, though not on Eric's plane of thought."

"Claire, I know you'll do a great job. Now, as well as getting started, and until we get premises, the second bedroom will be the office. The first priority is to secure premises, so a visit to the site is critical. My plan would be for us to turn up on our bikes to see the look on Pratt's face; that's the nickname I've given him. If we can get hold of drawings, together with plenty of photos, we can send that to Niall to prime him, and Fred to make a comparison with the YY video. Oh, cheers, everyone. I'm beginning to feel good. I think this must be the Chenin blanc."

"Absolutely right, and I, Ewan, trainee Master of Wine, can tell the difference from chardonnay. We'll all help with the admin as far as we can. Just tell us what you need and when. We'll work out a schedule for Niall covering not just the premises, but also the backbone of suppliers and sources of labour, and a possible architect and contractor for the refurb. Tom, is that okay with you?"

"Yup. We'll ask him for a list of the 'must sees'. It would help to ask Philip's brother to meet with him. By the time Niall is here, I hope to have a company credit card for each of us so there is no embarrassment with entertaining. We were treated royally in SA, so we need to respond in kind. Our nearest decent restaurant is Blacks, and I'll open an account. I'm looking forward to the fillet steaks. We won't be entertaining him in the uni canteen, and uni sandwiches are off the menu."

"Again, I can't speak for Eric, but I will. I'll have a secret peep at the property before we make formal contact with Pratt?"

"Thanks, Claire. Ewan, early next week would suit me. How about you?"

"I'm light on work at the beginning of the week, so, yes."

"Claire, if you want to contact Pratt and arrange a meeting, we can all pedal up in formation and make him double take. Feel free to mention that you might be happy with the stated price, and that moving the funds are always tricky times, but you would want a prompt response to any offer. As soon as we get a nod, or not, from Niall, we can move. Everyone happy?" There were glowing faces with nods all round like wicked schoolkids. "Ewan, you have a naughty look about you."

"That is my normal look. For me, I'm dying to see how the agent will react to our chief administrator as she asks the difficult questions. Fred's prep work will be essential reading, probably for us all. I'll tell him to make the comparison in size and facilities and anything else he expects we would need. Tom, it might be worth letting Mo know what we're up to."

"I will. Let's stop there and relax. Blacks has supplied our dinner. Ewan has taken control of this dining experience and has first-hand knowledge of sandwich placement."

Ewan shrugged his shoulders and whispered to Tom, "But what happens if all this goes 'tits up' and we're caught out. We don't have a plan B, but the robbers might."

CHAPTER 65

Bicycles at the ready, Tom led the way. Claire had arranged the appointment, and when 'Pratt' had asked whose secretary she was, she blasted him. "As a director," she said, "I prefer to operate my own diary." The put-down was increased when she added, "And are you the gofer?"

At the site entrance was a boy-racer BMW X1, with personalised number plates. Claire dismounted, propped her bike against the fencing and declared, "We're here. You must be 'Pratt'."

"I'm Stuart Ratt."

"So sorry, someone must have altered the sign. Please excuse me. Let's get going, we have more sites to visit. Can you confirm it is freehold and that apart from the encumbrance of the listed slipway, there aren't any other conditions?"

"Well, I'm not in a position to give you a legal view."

"But you are the seller's representative, aren't you? So, you must be au fait with the conditions. Should I be talking to the organ grinder?" The comment was lost on him. "Let's go."

It was as if Claire's dominance held him spellbound. Ewan thought of poor Eric. How much did he really know?

Relationships, as Ewan had discovered, were exciting but at times fraught. He would try and protect them both. They traipsed onto the site. Eric became attached to his camera, and Claire tried to keep the estate agent at bay. Tom and Ewan had their rosy specs on and everything they saw was perfect. Niall would be a realistic leveller.

As the session ended, Claire took the cue to disengage with the Parthian shot. "Seems doable. We'll let you know and will need our principal to visit and confirm our concerns."

"Sorry, what concerns?"

"Well, you quoted 'vacant possession', but there appears to be a sailing club encroaching on the territory. That will occupy our solicitor, and they cost money. We are after a simple sale with a short completion. If that can't happen, we wouldn't be interested."

"Oh, I'm sure there wouldn't be a problem. We have been down most avenues."

"We'll pass our investigations to our principal and possibly revert to you. Any offer we make would require a non-disclosure agreement and contain suitable headings to the offer. We would shy away from any restrictive covenants. You might wish to take a view from your superior in advance. We are working to a tight timescale. We have a narrow decision window. Thanks for your time."

Back in the "office", they started to relax and come off the high. "Claire, you were magnificent. I don't think he knew what hit him. We have enough ammo to send to Niall. Ewan, if you could ask Fred to email us the latest area development plan and the paperwork he has already found, we can scan and email the bundle to Niall. It'll give him time to pose any questions, and we can do the groundwork before he gets here. And Eric, if you could give us what you think are the best instructive pics, we'll add them in. After an enjoyably successful day as the 'famous five', okay 'four', let's celebrate with a dry chardonnay. Cheers, everybody."

With the others gone, the swap was made to Chenin blanc to decide the course of the evening. It helped them calm down and talk freely.

"You know I mentioned Fred had responded to my pics of the boat hulls and the 3 D printer, well he had asked what we were doing in SA, so I explained briefly the court case and the veiled threats to the company and why we might bring the equipment back. Almost by return and just like Fred, he had researched the trial and copied me the local *Cape News* extracts and the court proceedings with an article showing mugshots of the robbers. The piece was centred on the fact that they were a clan of drug dealers based in the northern townships and were renowned for the numbers of them who had already done time. From what I read, the sooner we get out the better. I didn't want to mention this in front of the others."

"That just adds confirmation that we're doing the right thing. I know you have a fondness for Fred, and he's helping, probably without knowing it. Sometimes, I wish I could give you what Fred gave to you."

"Look, Tom. Fred was all I had growing up, and, yes, I loved him, but not in the way I love you. I owe him for just being there. You, on the other hand, are my world and don't you forget it."

Tom and Ewan let the occasion take over the bed clothes. It was another declaration that they had picked one another as the only option. Ewan felt such warmth that made the image, body, and smell of Tom his only refuge. How could it stay that way? He would do anything to make it stick forever. As he urged sleep to let him rest, his brain kept insisting they were bound to step in a cowpat somewhere.

CHAPTER 66

By Wednesday, Niall's bundle was complete and dispatched. They had all worked hard to find the answers, while coping with their lecture schedules. Fred had been his usual meticulous self, and there was feedback from the estate agents. The waterline was defined on the council's maps, and there would be ample space to include a marina. The offices attached to the building were also listed as they abutted the slipway. But there was plenty of space and more, compared with the SA facilities. Mundane subjects such as sewerage and power supplies featured in the sales talk as both had been upgraded for the recent storage use. Claire had asked Niall what electricity the huge 3D printer used. The current occupants needed tremendous dehumidifiers, and they sucked up a large amount of power. They would just have to wait for Niall's visit, scheduled for the coming Tuesday.

Tom's computer pinged early on Friday morning before either had made it out of bed. Ewan pushed Tom out. "You'd better get that. If its Niall's response, we won't have much time to research and answer." And it was.

CHAPTER 67

"Ewan. While you were in the loo, Sarah called. Interesting chat. The upshot is that she and Jerry have decided to up sticks from SA and relocate to the UK. They've become paranoid with what could happen security-wise. She thinks the robbers' families are hell bent on revenge. Max is their world now, and she said she would do anything to protect him. I've never heard her so positive. I suggested she use Esk Hall, but they have decided they want to be in the South. Jerry wants to get into the pilot instruction game; he was an instructor before he joined BA. They don't need his huge salary. They're after quality of life. He's seen vacancies at a Bournemouth flying club: in fact, two clubs. He could provide input to our uni flying boat project. Anyway, it all points to living in our area, which would be great for us to watch Max grow up. We could be trainee daddies."

"Tom, I thought something like this might happen. I must confess that Sarah had asked me when you were out of their kitchen, what I thought about settling with you in the Southampton area, and I just said that wherever you are, I'm going to be. I think she started to cry."

"God, you're the best friend anyone could have. My sister and Jerry mean a lot to me, and now that Max is in the mix, they are part of my life, just as you are. I'd be happy to put down roots here. It would make a comfortable start. What do you think?"

"I don't care where we are. Let's agree that a flat here or a bothie in the wastelands of Scotland is all we need. The south coast holds bonds for us both and living here is as good a place as ever. It would be fun to get the family around us, and I say us, which makes me committed to what we want. If I think of Max, we can be family almost by proxy. Then, if we want to go down that route, we can boast experience. Changing nappies will be a first for us. I know you have a sensitive nose for smell."

"Ewan. I know my life is changing for the better, but if you could move your arse, I could relax more on my side of the bed. Why do you move so much at night?"

"Probably because I've always had some bedclothes to cover me. You seem to view the whole eiderdown as private property, and I can only get so much warmth from your exposed parts. Don't you ever wonder why I'm trying to cover you?"

"I thought you just wanted to feel me."

"Well, I do, but my backside needs to be warm too. We'll have to come to an arrangement, or get an over-sized duvet."

"Right. Tomorrow we visit IKEA. They have a solution for every domestic problem they say. Meanwhile, why don't we revert to the sleeping bag we used on that uni away-day at Southsea. That was the best closeness I have ever experienced. Remember, we were both out, yet still tightly in our comfort zones. I'll never forget how I felt."

"Well, I can hardly deny the part I played. I wish that

moment had gone on forever. Or has it?"

"It bloody has, and I want it to stay the same. All the bit players that come or go in our life need to stay at the edge. I want us to form a bond that no bastard can break. Mother Nature and our bodies will carry on, despite what we do, but the rest is down to you and me."

"Look, what I'm trying to say and get across to you is that I need you and your body, then I can face anything. Am I talking crap?"

"Nope.. When you think how far we've come in such a short space of time, we've struck gold, and I don't want to make any allusions to the SA heist. I'm ecstatic that Sarah wants to come here. You would be Max's uncle, several times removed."

"Well, I don't mind that, provided he stops pooping."

"Thanks. I have just entered hugging mood. Come here."

It was a beautiful moment that seemed to zero all their worries. They had done it before, and it was an unspoken way of reducing, minimising, or even killing their perceived problems.

"Ewan. Are you still awake?"

"Only just."

"I don't want to bore you, but I forgot to mention that I had a chat with my tutor about architects, and he said that they use a lecturer later in the course to cover the pitfalls of planning legislation and building regs in the company acquisition module. He's local to the uni but is well thought of locally. He has a book of contacts and even knows the chap who designed the BOAC museum and slipway for the council development area. He said it was, and still is, a masterpiece in glass and concrete, with, he said, 'a true and sympathetic treatment following the original drawings', and in those days, the Thirties, the visuals were stunning. Anyway, he is willing to make an introduction. What do you think?"

"Brilliant. We could ask Claire to do the legwork, 'cos she would also benefit from the contact."

"Great idea. She obviously enjoyed our first visit to the site. If we can get an architect to do a visit before Niall arrives, we'll be primed to answer any questions. I'll give Claire a ring."

"Now can I get to sleep?"

CHAPTER 68

There was an air of expectancy as they faced one another round the table in the "office". "Right, have we managed to answer all Niall's questions? I noticed that most of them were about water access. Did you action that, Ewan?"

"Claire asked me to do some delving, and I contacted the dock authority. They sent me this plan, which outlines who owns what and who can go where. To my unqualified eye, it looks good to me, and I scanned and sent it to Niall."

"And what about an architect?"

"That'll be me," Claire said putting her hand up like an excited schoolkid. "I've actually been on site with a chap recommended by my tutor's contact. His name is Roger Morrow, and he is on the edge of retirement, but loves a challenge. He described the BOAC museum alterations as his most fun job. He said it would be great to work for the 'modern young generation', as he put it, if we accept his retro-take on the building. I said our team might be on the young side but can do avant-garde. He seemed enthusiastic. We had Pratt again, but he was much more amenable this time, and Roger could talk right over his head. It was amusing to watch. I've written down all the questions he asked so when I do the buildings module, I'll have some of the answers already. I'm really into this project."

"Well, we should have enough info for Niall's visit, and if we can get the architect on site at the same time, that'll be a bonus." Tom sounded pleased. "Claire, you're a marvel."

"Oh, when I described who we were and what our aim was, his eyes lit up. He said he only lives in Southsea, and being semi-retired, he can be there when we want him. I mentioned costs, and he said they would be modest if he succeeds in designing something we like and get suitable publicity. He says there are a few of his contemporaries that he would like to upstage. I hope he gets on with Niall, and of course you, Tom."

"I'm all for adding modern to old. I'll get Mo at York Central to ask for his charges to put everything on a business footing. Ewan, can you think of anything we've missed?"

They continued the discussions including the mechanics of moving Niall around and hosting him. Ewan suggested they should get him a bike and use Uber for scouting the area if it rained. The air of optimism was evident.

CHAPTER 69

Smiling from ear to ear, Niall arrived at the Travelodge in a Bentley, courtesy of Mo the Arranger. Tom and Ewan were waiting. "That was very slick arrangements from the time I entered the Arrivals' Hall at Heathrow. Many thanks. When do we start?"

"We'll leave you to get settled in, and I suggest we meet again at about seven for dinner. We use a restaurant called Blacks just round the corner and within easy walking distance. Ewan and I can run through what we've learned and done to date. We've arranged to meet on site at ten o'clock tomorrow morning. It's quite close. We'll replace the Bentley with a different mode of transport to make it easier to get around tomorrow. We're glad you made it. See you later."

The dinner was a good-natured affair but Niall's update on the threat caused raised eyebrows. He said three of the staff had been dismissed for very poor workmanship, but which could have been construed as sabotage. The atmosphere at YY was changing. He was keen to explore all options.

CHAPTER 70

"Okay, Niall. Here's your transport. Sorry about the bright yellow colour, but it's a pretty sturdy bike. We'll only ask you to use it if the weather stays good. We're meeting the estate agent and the architect. Are you happy to cycle?"

"Sure. I need the exercise."

Claire led the way and exchanged greetings on arrival with her "friend" Pratt. It probably gave him something to talk about in the office when all these bikers turned up for a viewing. Claire made the introductions to Roger; he was with another chap whom he introduced as his brother Jeff, a retired surveyor. He said they were getting two for the price of one, and that Jeff could probably define what would and wouldn't work. Tom and Ewan held back to let the others feel more engaged with the project. It was two hours later with Pratt continuously looking at his watch when they re-met.

"Ewan. By the look of the smile on Niall's face, I think we may be onto a winner." Claire lowered her eyes demurely.

"Tom, you're right. Claire's been our star. She should take a bow. From what I've seen today, the questions Niall sent are being answered."

"You know me. Now, as a naturally inquisitive girl, I just happened to overhear Niall talking to Roger, and I heard the words, 'I'd be glad to receive instruction'. He said Jeff and him can produce outline plans within a week, providing the existing ground plan is accurate for sewage and contaminated ground. It all sounded so positive."

"When we re-group at the flat, I think Tom wants to be in a position to decide if he should make an offer. Claire, what do you think? I'm sure it would lighten Niall's load and give him a positive outlook when he gets back to SA."

"I'm up for it. In reality, as a group, we're living the dream of inventing something with no financial commitment from ourselves. Tom, you seem happy and that makes me feel good, and the project is moving up the exciting scale. I'm enjoying this."

"But you haven't mentioned Eric in the equation."

"Ewan. Let's just say that we are in a lovely bubble, helped by you lot. He knows he's superior on the water, and he knows I agree. And that makes us almost equal. I am amazed we get on, but we do. I don't think we would be together if it wasn't for Tom and yourself. It was probably what you didn't say that mattered, if that makes sense."

"Well, I think the heat will come on as actions take over from theory. Maybe Tom and I might ask too much of you both. Remember, we are a bunch of very close friends, privileged that we're in one another's confidence. Shout 'crap' if we're about to take a wrong turning or if our sums don't add up. Tom has assets that we'll need to commit to make this work, so don't be afraid to ask. I've only just stopped using Blue Stripe from Tesco. By the way, if anyone wants to know how long it would take for the RoRo to get here, it's about three weeks. Our timescales could be quite short, so it would be good to find out from Niall how long it would take to pack up in SA. I reckon the biggest task would be dismantling and loading the 3D printer – it's huge and heavy."

"And I forgot to mention that Sarah has an idea, if we have space on the site. She wants to use YY as a base for importing her wine for the UK and Europe. Niall has said there is ample room on the RoRo to take her entire current stock. I thought it would be fun and lift her spirits, pardon the pun. It would be a bonded store with Customs approval and full security precautions, so we won't just be able to pop in and re-stock."

"Pity. Can you imagine, Chenin blanc on tap? I can't think of anything better. I'm going to stay friends with Sarah. Though I'll have to keep an eye on Eric. I think it goes to his head quite quickly, and you know what that means."

"I can't say, though Tom's cheeks get flushed. It's fun to watch them both."

CHAPTER 71

They had just dropped Niall off at his hotel and were cycling back. "Tom, I think we should book a table at Blacks for dinner. The flat may be too personal to us for Niall to relax. After all, this could be a crunch meeting, although I'm optimistic."

"As ever, a good idea, then if it all turns to worms, we can disengage easily. That said, I've a good feeling like you, and the security situation in SA isn't going to get better anytime soon. This is going to be a momentous dinner, and I'm looking forwards even more to desert if you know what I mean."

"I couldn't possibly guess what you have in mind, but I know what I want for afters."

CHAPTER 72

Tom chose a table in the corner of the restaurant where they talked in hushed tones with the odd cackle of laughter. Claire's performance with Pratt came in for special mention. Ewan thought it must sound as if they were enacting a scene from the witches in Macbeth. With a hidden prod from Tom, Ewan took the initiative. "Niall. From what you've seen and heard, we're desperate to know if you've made up your mind about a possible move."

"Ewan, that's a difficult one to answer. My heart wants to me to stay in SA and beat the bastards who only want to create mayhem for their own political ends, but that would present serious challenges and, even then, it may not be possible to break their stranglehold on business. Now, my head says the opposite. SA is becoming too dangerous for the normal business activity to survive, except if we found a political backer or a dubious personality to deal with any fallout. YY has been a success story, and I think your dad would be pragmatic, and that is my take on what to do. Escape from SA and set up here seems the most sensible option. What I saw today, what you've discovered here, and my chat with Roger and Jeff leaves me feeling really positive. Roger made some brilliant suggestions, and Jeff put me at ease with his view of the site practicalities. And I must say, the research on water access was spot on. It's just what we would need. So, I guess it's up to you, Tom, to decide the way forward."

"Well, Claire has done excellent footwork and finding those two experts fills me with bags of comfort. I know there's lots of hurdles to get over, but everybody sitting here has been upbeat. My gut feeling is to go for it. Let's book the RoRo ferry for a one-way trip. Ewan. What do you think?"

"I'm too excited to give a reasoned response. But this is what we've been talking about. We need to make an offer on the site and get it accepted before we can move on."

"Niall, I'll get Mo to make a formal offer, then we have to sit on our hands until it is either accepted or rejected. You said that you were going to bring your departure forward because of the labour issue back in YY. That still gives us another day to criss-cross the area, so you get a feel for it. Claire's Roger said he can show you around the different industries here that could add to the sum total of your business knowledge were you to make the leap. And we can use an Uber to cruise the neighbourhood and check on housing and amenities. Let's go back to the flat and toast the future with Sarah's latest vintage."

CHAPTER 73

With Niall surveying the area, Claire and Eric in lectures, and Ewan and Tom in catch-up mode, the phones were in continuous use. Tom's phone rang again, and Ewan answered as Tom was still in bed. It was Mo. The gist of the conversation was that although they had thought of offering the base price, Mo discovered that the property had been touted on the market for three years. The car storage facility had been to fill a gap in the Council's coffers. Her initial discussion with the solicitors handling the sale pointed out the stagnation of the market and that there were other sites available, so her principal needed a swift decision. They answered promptly. Having offered four hundred thousand pounds under the base price of 3.5 million with no proviso of subject to survey, she knew there was a slight chance that there may be contaminated land that would need to be treated, which could always be a serious stopper in negotiations. Her declaration to make the offer with no riders offered the harassed council department an easy way out. They had accepted almost by return of post.

"Hullo. Are you awake yet?"

"Sort of."

"Well, that was Mo. The council have accepted your, or

should I say her offer, which was under the asking price. She is worth her weight in gold, though I don't know how much she weighs. I may have miscalculated the benefit. Anyway, we have a deal for the site. She will email the papers over and is in contact with Peter's solicitor brother. There is no chain involved, DocuSign is available, so completion is ready when you are."

"You are always good news. Why don't you come back to bed?"

"Get up. We have things to do and people to see. I'm excited. Once you are washed and clean, I'll show you how excited I can be."

CHAPTER 74

Niall came to the flat for breakfast featuring Scotch pancakes, topped with bacon and egg, a Ewan speciality. The only problem was that the smell of cooking always lingered, so the office and bedroom doors had to remain closed. It was substantial fare for the busy day they had planned. Niall was due to depart for Heathrow in the evening, and, having heard Tom's good news about the site, wanted to do a quick recce of the area for possible house options.

"We've booked your transport for the airport, but we have it here from ten this morning, and I hope you're not embarrassed, but it's the Bentley again. I expect you want to look upmarket anyway. Ewan has a stack of 'possibles' that he's downloaded from the internet. He followed your spec of looking at something with a view. So, we're aiming for the coast."

"You didn't give me a price range, so I went for three beds and a balcony, with no one overlooking. I discarded any with a swimming pool, as it costs a fortune to heat, but once you've picked a likely area, we can refine the search. We're also looking for Sarah as well, but we don't have any vineyards near here. Jerry wants to work down the coast at Bournemouth, so when she comes, we may have to throw the net wider. We assumed you would want to be near work."

"I think I need to be. This is not a simple project. I'll have to present a case for the move back home and use Ewan's research to convince the core team that the lifestyle will be enjoyable, despite the weather."

"Niall. Ewan and I have talked about funding and relocation expenses. As I said, we can afford to be very generous. Please remember I am trying to fulfil my dad's dream of a YY class of boat. That, and the fun of building YY in a new location, would be a dream come true. You're probably aware that Ewan and I are an item, and that we are happy to put down roots here. With Sarah and Jerry and the security situation, it all makes sense."

"I agree, and I've spoken to Karl, and his missus butted in to tell me they're going to move, and she doesn't care where as long as she can escape from SA. Karl then agreed enthusiastically. I don't see a problem with moving staff here, or finding new. From what I've seen, the unemployment state will help us, though we'll need to find workers who can work. I don't want to cast aspersions on UK workers, but I see Polish or Eastern European workers as a better bet. Ewan, maybe you can suss what the labour market is doing and let me know. I'll send you a list of trades we need to populate and the qualifications we need. It might help if I give you an updated video of our facilities, our latest brochure, specs, and an equipment list to help with recruiting. Operating the 3 D printer is fairly skilled and new. I'd bring our SA expert manager with us, if he'll come. Again, incentives might be crucial."

"The Bentley's here, Niall. This is exciting. As Sarah's

rep, I'm looking forward to this. And you, Ewan?"

"Well, I'm looking forward to the end of uni, so it's never too early to look for a flat replacement that doesn't have noisy neighbours. If you've had enough Scottish fare, let's go."

CHAPTER 75

The paperwork factory started up in earnest. Tom was inundated with legal tracts. With Niall gone, Ewan decided to try and take as much load as he could from Tom. Though Ewan's study schedule was exacting, he thought Tom's was a bit fuzzy, but didn't dare say so. It was fun following spreadsheet imperatives that all needed accurate answers. Niall's questions arrived in waves, and they followed a mechanical answering process that included Claire and Eric. It was amazing that the conversations continued when they sailed together. It was now a matter of not how, but when. The phone rang.

"Ewan, can you take that, I'm otherwise engaged.'

"Hello."

"It's Niall. Some important news. We've just had four of the black staff walk off the job. They said the work doesn't pay enough, but we know they get about thirty per cent above the average. One of our loyal guys says they are being manipulated by some firebrand in the Duggan clan who control much of what goes on in their Imizamu Yethu township, which is where the robbers came from. Karl, or more specifically his wife, wants to get out of here asap. The two yachts will leave for Dubai this week. The two new moulds have just completed. I've convinced everyone who matters that we are preparing the facilities to host a race, hence there will be lots going on. The RoRo is booked for thirty days' time, ostensibly to remove the printer for upgrade, and everyone seems to have accepted what we propose. All positive. We are on schedule for the move. Can't wait, and there might be a tenant for our facilities here. The reserve marine police detachment has been looking for a new home after getting torched last year. Tell Tom a nominal or very reasonable rent would secure the premises in more ways than one. It's still tentative and hush-hush until we can get an agreement, but I've been given the nod. The clan wouldn't be able to take possession. The police have learned their lesson after their dock also went up in smoke."

"I'll pass on the good news to Tom and get him to ring you with an update from this end."

Tom entered the kitchen looking troubled. "What's the matter? I've just had good news from Niall. We are good to go."

"I'm okay. I took a call from Mo earlier. She apologised for not getting in touch sooner about Mum and Dad. She said it hit her hard and found it difficult to come to terms with what Sarah and I would be going through. I told her about the court case and what we were trying to do. Graham had given her some info but thought it would be better if she spoke to me. She was crying down the phone. It was hard for me to appear positive and strong. Once you have your cup of coffee, I'll let you know what was said, and it's all positive."

"Thanks for that. You always brighten my day."

"The final part of my conversation with Mo concerned the purchase of the site and relocation of YY. She's told Graham that York Central will do all the spade work for the move and the contractual work with the estate agents, architect, surveyor and anyone else we must use. She was very insistent, so it should take quite a load off the team. She knows Niall well, and they get on. I didn't realise how much she enjoyed working with Dad. Norm will send me a DocuSign to transfer the funds to the seller's solicitors, via our solicitors. The conveyance should be completed by Friday of this week with vacant possession. We can then have a closer look at Urquhart's fence."

"There's always something that brings us down to earth. We seem to spend far too much time eagerly awaiting our next disappointment. But Mo's involvement all sounds positive. Let's chat with the team this evening. We both have a day of lectures. Why don't you treat us to your superb spag bol."

"Agreed. Now we better get going."

CHAPTER 76

The familiar ping-pong of the doorbell heralded the arrival of the rest of the committee. The kitchen table was loaded with all sorts of cheeses and the ever-present wine cooler. Ewan had lit some candles to create a party atmosphere and the wine glasses twinkled with their flames. The bol for the spag was simmering. The spag was eleven minutes from al dente.

"Thanks for coming round at short notice, but Ewan has some news for us, and some celebratory Chenin blanc. Help yourself. I took a call from Niall and all is set at their end. Apart from one or two staff problems, he's on schedule to wrap up the business in two months, that's the beginning of April when the RoRo ferry is due to dock at YY. Loading will take about a week, then the transit is roughly three weeks to here. The purchase of the premises should complete on Friday. That gives us almost three months to get the initial reception work done before its arrival. Claire, Tom will introduce you to Mo of York Central, the London office, and between you both, we can get the architect, the surveyor, and contractor moving. Niall has seen Roger's initial drawings and thinks the retro-look makes a great statement. What do you think, Tom?"

"The sketches he produced hark back to the old flying boat days and fit perfectly with the surrounds. The council planning department thought the same, so they just rubber-stamped it in committee. The full planning permission has been completed, and Mo is amazed they turned it around so fast. At first, she thought there was a catch, but when she spoke to the planning officer, they couldn't have been happier that we're going to revert to the old style with modern touches. When she mentioned dredging the dock area, he said it should have been done as part of the conditions while the Council were leasing the facility, so they will fix. All good news. Claire, can you act as our go-between with Mo and keep Niall up to speed? I don't know who we talk to about getting a ferry to dock at our premises."

"We haven't covered docks and harbours yet; we're still at restrictive clauses, covenants, and rights of way in the planning module, but my tutor is bound to know which button to press. I'll report back when I have an answer. Now, can you please give Eric more work to do as he won't leave me alone; whoops, I mean in my capacity as YY gofer."

"I don't interfere. I only make suggestions from a distance looking at the bigger picture. You certainly don't need any help dealing with Pratt. Maybe Tom will let you loose on Urquhart when the time comes."

"Definitely, but I hope you two are enjoying the challenge. Ewan keeps me on track, and it's fun to make suggestions that come out of leftfield but end up solving a problem. Let's face it, the RoRo was Ewan's idea."

"I don't take all the credit. If we hadn't been round the Cape, courtesy of Niall and his team, I would never have spotted the ship. I think it's called happenstance or serendipity, not the ship I hasten to add, but not sure which applies to my intuitive skills. My other aim is for Sarah to load all her stock on board. If she does, we'll have the band playing the Drinking Song on the dockside when it arrives. Let's drink to that."

CHAPTER 77

"Tom, I've just had an email from Niall. He's also sent a video on dismantling the huge printer and transferring the stock. They had to work overnight to meet the departure timing. I've sent the video to Fred to whet his appetite on the moulds. The ferry left an hour ago, fully laden. He says he's going to brief the staff as to what's actually happening. He expects a rough ride, but the latest security skirmishes in the area gives him sufficient ammo, metaphor intended, to justify his action. The list of those wanting to transfer to the UK is now ten, so he has asked us to set up rental accommodation for four families and six singles. He has his eye on one of the houses we saw with him and has already made an offer. Karl has also almost committed to a flat to start with. He is using the website to find suitable long-term accommodation for the others. It's all systems go. Now we have to get as much prep done as we can to receive YY. Did you say that Norm is coming over this week?"

"Yes, and you've got to be here. We've a lot of ground to cover. You'll like his positive approach. We need to think long term and give him some steers to organise the finances. It may be that we only charge the new YY a nominal rent. We have a fifty-one per cent share in the business, so we are going to pay tax whichever way we go."

"Tom, you keep using 'we', but it's your inheritance, your money, not mine; I can't, and shouldn't have a say in what to do."

"My fault. I want you to. There might be a solution to our problems. In the meantime, I need all your help to stay afloat with what is happening. You protect me. I can't ask anything more. Do you understand?"

"Of course I do. I'll try and take as much weight off your shoulders as I can. Just say when."

"Right. First off, there are some potential UK clients that Niall suggests we meet. We'll need to make an effort in smartness

"Wednesday is free for study. How about you?"

"Right. I can do Wednesday. I'll tell them eleven o'clock. We'll meet at their legal office. You never know, we might be onto a winner. My fingers are crossed. Just remember to say the right things."

"I hope I always do."

CHAPTER 78

"Tom, do I look smart enough? I thought the striped soft-colours tie should put them at ease."

"Oh, it will, I'm sure. The taxi is here. A hug to go?"

Settled into the back, Ewan thought Tom was very relaxed for what he described was to be a crucial meeting. He had no business cards as they were still being printed, and the literature on YY was now out of date. "Where exactly is the meeting?"

"We're about five minutes away according to my all-seeing watch. I've never used its tracking feature before. The building in their bumph didn't look imposing, but I suppose it's what's inside that's important. Gee, I think we're here."

This looks like the Town Hall."

"So it is. Let's get out here."

"I thought you said it was a nondescript building."

"I think we have to go in a side door. Yes. Here it is."

"But that says, 'Registrar of Births, Deaths, and Marriages'."

"Just shut up and go in." Tom then led through another door into a kind of waiting room with wood-panelling walls and vases of flowers everywhere. Already seated were

Claire and Eric.

"What are you two doing here?"

"Well now that you ask, we're waiting for you." Ewan looked at Tom whose face was just one big smile.

"Ewan, remember when two rings just happened to appear. Well, two can play at that game, and now it's my turn. Look, your tie isn't done up properly. It needs to be for this, our big day." The truth dawned on Ewan, and he too started to smile.

"You bugger, you might have told me."

"What, and spoil the surprise. Let me show you something you should recognise." Tom pulled at his neck chain, the one Ewan had revealed on the yacht, and attached to it were two gold bands. "Look, one for me and one for you, just as you did ages ago."

"Was that why you were comparing hand spans when you were actually checking my finger size?"

"Might have been, but I hope I guessed correctly." The door at the far end of the room opened, and Ewan caught strains of Wagner's "Ride of the Valkyries". It was all falling into place. Before Ewan could accost Tom, they were invited into a grand hall, again with plenty of vases of flowers. Ushered to two grandly upholstered chairs, Tom pushed a reluctant Ewan towards one, and he took the other. The service was short and sweet, with no religious elements. The Registrar seemed to go out of her way to make them welcome and put them all at ease. Ewan still had butterflies in his tum. He managed to recite the lines he was given without fluffing, and Tom placed the gold band on the correct finger. Ewan made as if he didn't know which of Tom's fingers was the right one. They all laughed when

Tom took charge. It was a special moment for Ewan and his grin widened till it hurt. She declared them husband and husband and the kiss and hug he received from Tom was the best ever. He had to hold back very emotional tears, not helped by Claire blubbing almost silently behind. Then, as if by magic, the strains of Borodin's *Mongolia* started up, with the pictures of the Siberian steppes intruding on their minds. Ewan looked at Tom. Both Wagner's and Borodin's music harked back to Esk Hall and made a poignant memory moment.

With the paperwork complete, they exited into wonderful sunshine with Tom stating, "What a difference a day makes, and I think I speak for us both. Thanks, Claire and Eric. That meant a great deal to both of us. Now to Blacks for lunch, and Ewan can undo his tie a little." They made a noisy arrival at the restaurant. Eric was keen to get photos of the couple standing in the restaurant's ornate carved entrance that had once ushered in the great and the good to deposit their ill-gained cash. It had been the Brook Bank until the Great Crash. Now its vestibule welcomed the elite and well-healed cognoscenti who valued superb food in its magnificent mahogany setting. The soft carpet as they entered brought the noise level down. They trooped in behind the Maitre'd.

CHAPTER 79

The staff at Black's were in the know and had laid their favourite alcove table with a sparkling white linen tablecloth – not a beer mat in sight – and rose petals and green garlands made a grand statement. The lunch was a merry affair with toasts to everyone. When Tom said," You're next," Claire blushed as bright as a berry. She made a little speech thanking Tom for introducing them to one another and the unusual friendships that had taken over. Eric looked up at the ceiling. They all laughed. It was a fun day, with the morrow promising just as much. The plan was for them all to go aboard *Scarborough Fair* the following day, with a trip round the Isle of Wight as a practice honeymoon. Rob Iveson, an old school friend and an accomplished sailor, had agreed to skipper the run.

As Ewan and Tom reached the flat, neither could decide who should go first. "Tom, you should carry me over the threshold."

"No. You made the first proposal possible; I only consecrated it into marriage by calling the Registry office."

"Right, I'll carry you over, but don't wriggle." They fell into the flat and hugged. "Tom, thanks for today. I loved the music, and Claire and Eric were just the right people to be our witnesses. How long have you been planning it?"

"Ever since you talked about not being able to provide a Max. It churned me up inside, and it was a moment I'll never forget. I knew then we had to be together permanently, come what may."

"Well, I haven't felt this good since Mum and Dad told me I was an only child because they couldn't make a better one than me, and I believed them. Now I'm in agreement with you, and I can't believe my luck though I'm wiser now. Just remember, it was your eyes that did the talking. Let's call Sarah and tell her, with a glass of Chenin blanc in our hands; I feel I'm now one of the family. Then we can go to bed. I have lots of things to say to you, and bed seems the best place."

CHAPTER 80

Underway on the yacht with a testing breeze to keep them on their toes, Tom was in his element, and they quickly settled into their sailing routine and allocated jobs. Ewan, as principal sheet-puller, reacted to whoever shouted the loudest with suitable rude replies. Tacking into a Force 6 with short bursts of going about kept everyone alert and ducking. As the swell took on a mind of its own, Ewan punched Tom on the shoulder when they collided to emphasise what had just happened. The others looked on with smiles of encouragement. It was a suitable celebration ending neatly at the marina with all hands helping. They had sailed round the Isle of Wight, anchored in a small bay for lunch, then motored slowly back up the Solent. Ewan spoke standing on what they called the Captain's Potty, a platform close to the forward gunwales. "Days like this don't come much better. I just want you all to know how much I, and probably my husband, appreciate you giving generously of your time."

Claire opened her arms and blew a kiss. "Think nothing of it. Rob and I go way back to secondary school time, and he owes me for telling him about two-timing Rosie, and before you get upset, Eric, he already has a firm girlfriend.

But what you don't know is that we re-met in the uni canteen last week, and we talked about Operation Seahorse. Rob, do you want to give them your suggestion?"

"Right. When I knew Claire, I used to boast that my dad knew Southampton Waters better than anyone else 'cos he was a harbour pilot. I've sailed all my life; he made sure of that. He's now the Master Pilot and is best mates with the Harbour Master. Well, when your RoRo arrives here, it'll need shepherding, and it can be a costly business. I mentioned it to Dad, and he suggested they might use their monthly tugboat drill to help it in. They practise what's called the 'Dockers' Ballet' minus tutus. The idea is to simulate taking either an underpowered ship or one with broken bow thrusters and dock them safely. So, the offer is there when your ship arrives. It receives good publicity, and a RoRo would present an ideal challenge. They would survey your dock, its approaches, and depths available. That's it. What do you think?"

"Sounds a brilliant idea," Tom said enthusiastically and gave Claire a hug. "Eric, you have a treasure there with all her contacts."

"Please don't get her more big-headed. I have enough to put up with as it is. I must say it'll give us and Niall comfort that the arrival will be in such good hands. Rob, nearer the time, it would be worthwhile meeting your Dad and the Harbour Master. Niall will be here by then and will be able to prepare the slipway and surfaces for the 3D machine. It's heavy and massive, but it looks like there'll be enough room to get the off-loading crane into position. It'll pay to check. Ewan, you've walked the ground with the surveyor and the contractor. Did they say the ground will take the crane?"

"Yes. They've drilled bore holes in the current concrete hardstandings, and the base for the printer is being prepared with reinforced rods. The only issue is rolling the unit into place, but they have some clever pneumatic lift bags. Niall can double-check when he gets here. It's going to be an exciting day for all of us. Maybe we should sell tickets, or get the local TV station involved. It would make good PR for YY, unless it all goes tits-up – apologies Claire."

"You boys can be so juvenile with your language. Next time you hear me swear, don't give me that pained look. There is a time to be lady-like and a time not to be. Isn't that right, Eric?"

CHAPTER 81

Since Niall's arrival, Ewan and Claire had spent long stints going over the reception details for the RoRo's docking. Apart from the weather, Ewan felt they had all bases covered. In discussion with Rob's dad, the only problem he could foresee was the wind element as they came up the main channel. Where they would make a tanker stand-off if they were unhappy, they couldn't afford to lose the window of the tug availability. But he said they liked a challenge, especially as the channel narrowed substantially round the second gore. The RoRo was due to arrive from the west at the Needles at just after first light in three days' time.

Ewan and Tom were checking on the clean-up at the deep-water berth when Ewan's phone pinged. "It's an email from Fred." Ewan's eyes grew wider and wider. "Fred has viewed Niall's latest video and found infrared coverage at the end of the video. It looked like security camera footage, and Fred thinks it could be sabotage. He says there's a chap unscrewing the underfloor hatch of the printer and loading dozens of packages into the gap. He says he counted a hundred and two. He saw the guy replace the cover then spread what looked like white liquid over the floor, which Fred said would be black in normal light. He also says they

262

have filled some of the barrels with the same-sized packages, which looked odd to him. He didn't think it was normal, but said he isn't familiar with 3D printers. Tom, what do you think we should do?"

"Let's call Niall and get him to review the video." Niall responded almost immediately and talked as he watched the playback. He recognised two of the individuals, and said the packages were almost certainly drugs and the liquid most probably made to resemble an oil leak. The individuals are probably on board. He would let the police know and get them to take action. He suggested it may be possible to divert the RoRo en route and escort it to its original destination of St Nazaire, where they could offload the drugs quietly under Gendarmerie supervision, detain the potential smugglers, then UK police could board at sea and wait for the planned pick-up. He would set the wheels in motion. Tom and Ewan shook their heads in disbelief. "And we thought our plan was fairly watertight, and I don't use that word lightly. It all seemed so smart and simple in the beginning …

Niall called back later in the evening. When Tom's phone rang, they both looked at one another, shaking their heads expecting the worst. The captain had been informed and the ferry would declare an engine emergency when closest to St Nazaire, its original destination. Escorted in, the ferry would be searched and made clean by police, substituting fake packages, then leave for Southampton. Once police had examined the imagery, the two suspects had been identified as members of the Duggan clan. Niall recognised them as the trouble makers that had walked off the job. Locked up without their mobiles, they would be unable to reveal what was happening. The UK police had already been informed and would keep the ferry under constant surveillance. It seemed a workable plan. Niall rang off with a resigned sigh.

"Right, Tom. It's out of our hands, but my level of excitement and dread has just rocketed in equal measure."

"Me too. We'll have to keep this to ourselves and watch how the plot unfolds. I wonder who will try and pick-up the fake drugs. They'll get a warm reception."

CHAPTER 82

The weather was misbehaving at first light. The wind was gusting twenty knots, which would enliven the dockers' ballet. The RoRo had reached Southampton Water and was due to move up the Solent and enter the Itchen River at Dock Head about nine o'clock. The pilot was already aboard, as were the police surveillance team, and the tugs were lined up abeam Ocean Dock. Ewan and Tom had plotted a route for their driver so they could see the arrival at the river entrance with sufficient time to return to YY. Eric had the PR side covered by arranging for a video expert to film the arrival at the Needles from a drone; then the same company would follow the RoRo's progress up the Itchen.

"Mike, we can stop in the Ocean Terminal car park. I called ahead, and we can go onto the Roof Restaurant balcony to see the stately progress up the river. I'm bloody excited. This is the old BOAC building that Roy brought up to date with plenty of glass, as you can see. YY's refurbishment reflects this retro feel. What do you think?"

"This place looks and feels the business. When you think the high and mighty detrained here, had a sumptuous meal, then boarded either a transatlantic liner or a tremendous boat-plane. What a lifestyle." As they arrived in the upper restaurant, the sun had popped out. "Roy was right about the burred walnut; there's acres of it here. I thought he was overdoing it at YY, but when I see it here, the quality says it all. God, look. Here it comes, and it's huge. Those red funnels on either side must allow the middle to be used as a flat road. The front looks too heavy and high, and the back is an enormous wide plank. I suppose practicality took precedence over aesthetics. It's much, much bigger than I thought and only just fits on the river. I hope the dredger work is sufficient. The tugs seem tiny in comparison with their stubby bows. We owe Steve a drink for his dad's contribution. To think our hopes and plans are chugging along at five knots right past our noses. We better take the pics and scoot."

The arrival back at YY left plenty of time to take in the view, not just with the myriad of ants scurrying about, but also the public that had come to share the experience, not to mention a nondescript team of police and customs officers dressed in boiler suits with nothing to do. The tugs were busy cajoling the big ship to get its pointed end between the two docks. It was truly a ballet as the River Itchen seemed to have another idea. Several toots showed exasperation, and long blasts back felt like rebukes. Ewan and Tom stood next to the dockside office watching the team under Niall's supervision throw the lead ropes to obtain the hawsers. "Tom, I'm having a flashback to when I threw you the lead rope to secure you in my life. Is that too poetical?"

"No, it's just right and makes me feel good. We've come a long way and so has the RoRo. Bloody hell, is that Sarah up there at the rail? It effing well is, and she's with Jerry and Max, and she's waving. I hope they don't drop Max in the excitement. She kept that a secret."

"Not exactly, but I thought I wouldn't let on, though it's been hard to keep my mouth shut."

"You, bastard. You kept shtum all this time. I could have made arrangements for their reception and accommodation."

"No need. It's all been sorted. You've already seen their house; it's just that you didn't know that. It was the one you liked that had the balcony sea-view, and a sandpit in the garden for Max. They bought it sight unseen, except for me and now you. It was fun keeping the secret from you. You can thank me later. Oh, there goes the long toot to say 'finished with engines'. YY now has its bits and pieces alongside. We should sell tickets to watch the tricky offload. Let's go meet and thank everyone."

"And you didn't bloody tell me. I'll remember that."

"But Sarah swore me to secrecy as she wanted to surprise you, as well as escorting her own wine."

CHAPTER 83

Ewan and Tom decided the upstairs office would give the best view of the loading area, as did the police who had set up surveillance cameras; they didn't have long to wait. The drug runners probably expected to pick up their consignment in the confusion of the arrival, and, sure enough, three men dressed in white overalls were spotted examining the printer base as it sat on the dock-head. They had parked a van just to the rear of the slipway entrance. In the surrounding chaos, one of them started to move some barrels to the dock as if on a delivery, while the other two unscrewed part of the printer's floor. The policeman standing at the office window kept up a running commentary using his binoculars. The runners were an efficient trio, and about half the suspect packages were into the barrels and on their van in minutes, and one of them was retrieving barrels that had been strapped to the printer uprights. The police moved in to block the van, and under the watchful eye of a very keen Alsatian, they were handcuffed in short order. The ferry tooted twice to indicate "mission accomplished". The inspector in charge of the team standing next to Ewan and Tom punched the air, so the pair of them did likewise. He said they had been trying to nab these narcos for ages, but they always seemed to get tipped off, so these arrests would bolster morale. The connection with South Africa had been uncovered just in time by Fred's discovery, and the smugglers on the RoRo had been identified as belonging to the Duggan Clan. Niall had been able to send mugshots to the French authorities to secure their arrests, and the SA detectives wanted to thank his source. Niall didn't want to involve Fred, but agreed to forward a commendation certificate once the dust had settled. Ewan was chuffed by the gesture, and Tom said he would get it suitably framed in burr walnut - to mark a special occasion.

The RoRo ferry had done its job. The 3 D printer would be up and running soon. The two moulds were sitting on their cradles waiting for the technicians to get to work. With the computers tied to the cloud, all systems were go, and the bonded store would be brimming full with Sarah's wine. The suite of offices had the retro look, and Niall was very pleased with the reception area and boardroom. There were still external touches to finish.

Eric called a 'board' meeting to show his PR handiwork, so a lunchtime session evolved into back-slapping, hand-shaking, and head-nodding with expressions of satisfaction. To have foiled a drug plot was the icing on the cake, and all due to Fred's vigilance.

They watched the stately departure of the RoRo and dancing tugboats, the latter using their horns to mark a memorable day. The toast was 'YY' and Fred. Eric's video of the arrival and offload recorded a fascinating triumph of serendipity over dark forces with the drugs sting making it all the more eventful. Even the custom's officer allowed a test session on the imported wine, and he, too, was partial to Chenin blanc.

They all agreed, with the help of the latest vintage, that now was the time to confront Urquhart.

CHAPTER 84

This final part of the YY jigsaw was to remove the thorn next door. The plan was to block off the entrance to the snooty club, then wait for a reaction. Claire had done her homework, and Philip's brother Jim, the solicitor, had been happy to meet and brief the team. Fred's investigation of site boundaries, coupled with the planning application the sailing club had to make to get approval for their building extension, meant that they had only squatted on the access roadway for three years. The council, who owned the land, admitted they didn't know about the hoarding that the sailing club had erected at the road leading to their car park; it hid the change the club had made to their entrance. The previous fence had been removed. Solicitor Jim said a person seeking adverse possession must be "open and notorious" meaning they must occupy a parcel of land that is open and obvious, whereas hiding their handiwork suggested the opposite. He had drafted a formal notice to the club asking them to remove all their fence-work off YY land. He made it quite a punchy letter with suitable legalese, and plenty of mapping and documents from the council's archive. They all read it. His advice was to reassert their legal possession if the sailing club didn't move off YY land. He also mentioned that YY could offer an encroachment or wayleave to the club but gain something in return. "Basically, you have a ransom strip, and they will, or should, now know that."

CHAPTER 85

As ever, they sat round the table in the flat. Their only agenda item was the ransom strip. Ewan was the first to speak. "Look, as we have to live together, we can give them access, and in return I suggest our board gets honorary memberships. That would be my 'quid pro quo', and I hope it would get right up Urquhart's nose, and I don't even speak Latin." Claire couldn't stop laughing. The others looked at Ewan in amazement. "And to prove our point, we can erect our own fence on our own land to obstruct their car park access and establish our rights and watch the car queue build up. Then we agree to a face-to-face meeting with his committee. I'll learn proper land-associated Latin phrases to sound knowledgeable. Claire can do the talking. I'll butt in with my erudition. How about that?" Nobody disagreed. Jim was to set the ball rolling with suitable paperwork.

Almost by return, Jim received what amounted to a squatters' rights declaration, or what he called "adverse possession rights" statement. Niall arranged for YY's boundary fence to be in place before the weekend.

Tom took a call from the Secretary's secretary, suggesting a meeting to "resolve our current issue". They agreed to attend, including Niall, and listen to any proposal they offered. Everyone was excited and agreed that Claire would take the lead for YY, which they felt would get up Urquhart's nose even more.

Shown into a very sumptuous boardroom, where an oak forest must have been slaughtered to provide the backdrop, the five of them took their seats opposite the Secretary, the Secretary's secretary, and a pince-nezed individual who looked legal. A rather large gentleman sat centre-stage, overflowing his seat. Introductions were brief, revealing that the fat individual was the President of the club.

Urquhart opened the proceedings. "The fence you have erected is stopping our members accessing our car park. It has to come down. *Uti possidetis*, which, if I recall my Latin correctly, means 'as you possess, so may you continue to possess'". The team looked to Claire.

"That's very interesting. I'm afraid my Latin is a trifle rusty. Forgive me if I run over some detail that you ought to know already. You are in adverse possession of our land, and according to all the documents we have accessed, including historical aerial photos, and a boundary surveyor's report, and referring especially to the 2002 Act, you are, pardon my pun, on shaky ground. You have never registered what you think you own, bearing in mind you must be aware the freeholder was, at the time, the local council. Even if you applied to exercise what is vulgarly addressed as squatters' rights, you are now out of time and out of right. We have made challenge, which you cannot re-butt. Putting it bluntly, you are in the shit. Sorry for my language, but, as I said before, my Latin is wanting. I need to make the point bluntly, so we don't start skating round the problem." The team stifled as many laughs as they could. Eric's face was bright red.

Ewan decided to fill the embarrassing lull in responses. "Before you say anything more on any relationship we may have with your club, I remember from my Latin days at school, the words '*Nemo me impune lacessit*'. Mr Urquhart, you'll remember the Scottish wording, I'm sure. But for everyone else, it means 'Don't meddle with me'. You shouldn't presume to treat us as young, inexperienced, and naïve. Our collective knowledge is various and covers many disciplines, and believe you me, we have done our homework. Your President may have a view or suggestion to offer."

"Yes. We seem to be at odds with you," he said as he turned and stared at Urquhart. "Does your company have any suggestions how we may come to an understanding?"

Claire resumed the dialogue. "We might suggest that in return for a right of way, you would consider offering the five officers of the YY board honorary membership of your club for as long as the arrangement suits both parties. Our aim is to establish a business at the upper end of sophistication in the yachting business world, as we did in Cape Town. Our standards are second to none. We would need an agreement in principle before we depart this meeting if we were to remove the boundary protection. What do you say?"

The President got up and stood behind his chair. "Well, this has been a revelation to me. I hope we haven't given the impression that we are stuck in the old traditions. We tend to move slowly with the times, and I think that makes us attractive to our membership. But we need to be pragmatic, and your suggestion has merit. What do you think, Mr Urquhart?" Urquhart's mouth opened and closed like a fish in an aquarium. The President continued. "While I have a duty to consult my committee, I aim to proceed on the basis you have suggested, and if your solicitor can draft some terms along the lines discussed, I believe we can settle our differences. I look forward to welcoming you to our club. It may be that once you are fully established, we can discuss joint ventures. As you can see, our marina is quite full, so a reciprocal arrangement with yourselves could be an advantage to us both." He nodded towards Urquhart saying, "I'm sure our Secretary will move with pace to make the necessary arrangements."

Tom responded with a nod of his head. "Rest assured we have both of our best interests at heart, and we'll work at speed on our part. The access fence will be repositioned today. I would just add that our present build of the YY 50 has been offered as a new class of yacht to the Sailing World body for approval, and it is at their committee stage. You may consider this location would be a suitable launch venue. We are also on track to use our prototype composite facilities and slipway to develop an electric seaplane, so we will be at the cutting edge of progress. We live in exciting times, yet appreciate what made this area great. When you think of it, the BOAC seaplanes that operated from here set a brilliant precedent for us all. We call our project 'FRED', Flying boat Re-engineered for Electric Drivetrains, which we aim to design at uni. It's perfectly placed to respond to the current push for green electric aircraft. It should give this backwater a lift and identity." The President's face became a picture of incredulity. "But, of course, retaining the historic feel," Ewan hastened to add.

With much false smiling, the team made it into the

fresh air, and as they turned the corner of the building, they all punched the air. It was game, set, and match. Urquhart's face had been an absolute picture as Claire took her leave of the President.

CHAPTER 86

"Ewan, you amaze me. Where did all that Latin come from? I didn't think you were that well-read," Tom said gleefully. "I'm glad I can always surprise you. Our secondary school had a Stuart lineage, and all our bloody exercise books had their motto on the back in large print you couldn't miss, which just happens to be *'nemo me impune lacessit'*. There was also a huge badge with a lion rampant, which we coloured in to give it the worst look possible you can imagine, and, of course, we made the lion truly 'rampant'. Underneath all this was the Scottish translation from the Latin, *Wha daur meddle wi' me*. Unfortunately, somebody added some wording to Tina Hopkin's exercise book; it read, 'cos if you do, you'll get VD'. Despite her being the tart of the class, she complained to the teacher, and when the class was challenged to find the culprit, no one owned up, so all us boys received a week's detention, save Fred as he pleaded ignorant to what it all meant. His exchange with the teacher was hilarious, which only made it worse for the rest of us. When I tried to explain it later to Fred, all he said was, 'I looked up VD, and it's quite infectious, so it was a good warning'. Tom, that Latin phrase will be forever with me, just as I hope you will."

"What about '*semper simul, quid impedit*' for us?"

"Depends what it means. My Latin is very limited as you know."

"It means 'together forever, come what may', if that's not too sentimental. My dad had it on the family crest. Little did he know how apt it would be for Sarah and me when both of them were taken together. The thought makes me shiver."

"No, it isn't too sentimental. Come here. Let's stop you shivering. It reminds me too much of the malarial effects back in Bermuda. We've been through a lot, and I couldn't be happier right now."

"Okay. When we've recovered from this latest episode on our unimaginable journey, why don't we take a trip to Invergordon. You've done my Yorkshire dales; I can do your Scottish hills, and I would love to meet Fred. Wouldn't you?"

"Tom, I would. Coming from you, you'll never know how special that suggestion is. You always say the right words, but we have mountains, not hills."

The end ... I think.

Printed in Great Britain
by Amazon

78030625R00164